KNIGHT SIR LOUIS

THE DREADFUL DAMSEL

Praise for *Knight Sir Louis and the Dreadful Damsel*!

'Dazzlingly silly and brilliant fun.'
Matt Brown, author of *Compton Valance*

'The Brothers McLeod's scratchy penmanship and casual
attitude to the conventions of story-telling spin the fairy
tale in a new direction, as if Hans Christian Andersen had
cornered you in a pub and got his own yarn in the wrong
order, or The Brothers Grimm had squeezed up next to you
with a Tupperware box of home-made sandwiches on a long
coach journey. Knight Sir Louis is an epic non-epic saga.'
Stewart Lee, comedian

'A scampering, walloping fantasy adventure, brimming with
ludicrous magic and fizzing with irresistible comedy.'
Peter Lord, co-founder of Aardman Animations

'Probably the funniest book I've ever
read. A masterclass in silliness!'
Gary Northfield, author of *Julius Zebra*

'This is a really funny book, and will appeal to
anyone who likes adventures and laughing.'
Philip Reeve, author of the *Mortal Engines* series

'Sublime daftness on every page.'
Jeremy Strong

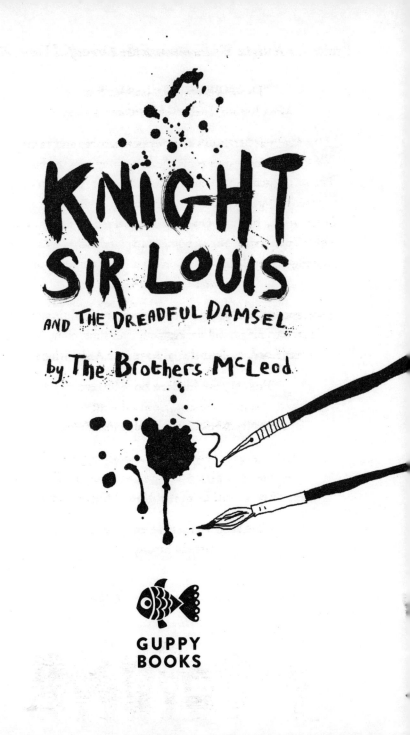

KNIGHT SIR LOUIS

AND THE DREADFUL DAMSEL

by The Brothers McLeod

**GUPPY
BOOKS**

KNIGHT SIR LOUIS AND THE DREADFUL DAMSEL
is a GUPPY BOOK

First published in 2020 by
Guppy Books,
Bracken Hill,
Cotswold Road,
Oxford OX2 9JG

GUPPY PUBLISHING LTD Reg. No. 11565833

A catalogue record for this book is available from the British Library.

Typeset in 13½/20 pt Adobe Garamond by
Falcon Oast Graphic Art Ltd, www.falcon.uk.com

Printed and bound in Great Britain by CPI Books Ltd.

For Louis

KNIGHT SIR LOUIS

The young hero of this tale. A calm and clear-thinking champion in a bonkers world. All the most difficult quests are entrusted to him. His name is pronounced "Loo-ee".

CLUNKALOT

The trusty mechanical steed. Sturdy, brave and always ready to join his beloved master Louis on a dangerous quest. Also loves flying and poetry.

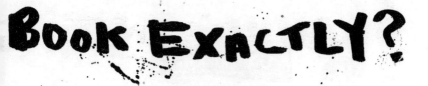

BOOK EXACTLY?

MR CATALOGUE

This boar is a unique sort of piggywig. Loyal, willing to try anything once (or even twice), with a brain made "much more thinky" by magic.

PEARLIN

A young, self-taught wizard and inventor (or wizentor!). Always coming up with new and fun ways of using machines and magic.

KING BURT THE NOT BAD

The (mostly) kind and (usually) fair King of Squirrel Helm who lives in Castle Sideways.

DAVE THE SWORD

A magical sword recycled from a magic mirror. Likes reflecting magical spells, chopping up nasty things and singing. (Is an awful singer.)

MYSTO

The greatest wizentor ever known. Used to be good but turned evil for some mysterious reason.

CHAMPION TRIXIE

A wise, champion knight who is always busy defending, organizing or partying. Also . . . she's Knight Sir Louis' mum.

A fiendish, giant knight with stripy armour. Who's hiding inside? No one knows!

CHAPTER 1

4

CHAPTER 2

Well, wasn't Chapter One ridiculous? Let's start again. This is a proper Chapter One, though now we'll have to call it Chapter Two because of all that nonsense in Chapter One. Anyway, here we go . . .

This is the story of Knight Sir Louis.

HOORAH!

STOP THAT!

Knight Sir Louis is the bravest of all knights in all lands. Braver than Knight Sir Colin in the bogs of Wattasmel. Braver than Knight Sir Barbara in the mountains of Itso-Hy. Even braver than Knight Sir Gary from the soggy lands of Tippinitdown.

COLIN   BARBARA   GARY

Being brave is what Knight Sir Louis is known for.

But Louis is modest. He says he's not brave, but just good at staying calm when everyone else is going completely bonkers.

When he was a little boy the local lord locked himself out of his horse-drawn double-decker bus. It was bad timing as the lord was supposed to be going to the Royal Wedding. The lord and lady and all their friends were very upset and running around in a panic. But little Louis, only four years old, spotted they'd left a window open. He simply reached inside and unlocked the door. It turns out this kind of clear thinking is useful if you need to defeat hungry dragons, evil goblins and horrible wizards. And that's why King Burt appointed him defender of the great Castle Sideways.

OK, so now you're wondering who is King Burt and is his Castle Sideways really sideways? Well, one thing at a time . . .

King Burt is the ruler of a kingdom known as Squirrel Helm. I know it's a silly name. Don't look at me. It's not my fault! Anyway, King Burt is a good king. I don't mean he's brilliant. He's not amazing. He's all right, you know? He is known to his people as King Burt the Not Bad. (He's certainly better than his dad who was known as King Larry the Hostile.)

Burt comes from a long line of kings and queens. Here are some of them: King Alan the All Right, Queen Olive the OK, Prince Ned the Ninny-Winny and Empress Sissy the So-So.

King Burt's favourite hobbies are giving speeches, throwing banquets and playing computer games. Yes, computer games. He's really good at them, especially the one where you have to race a horse and cart around a land full of giant toadstools and stuff.

Of course, just because King Burt is a good(ish) king doesn't mean he's always fun to be around.

Before Knight Sir Louis, the king's champion was Knight Sir Trevor. He was brave and noble, but one day he failed to stop the double-headed dragon Borax from eating King Burt's brother, Prince Garibaldi (famous for smelling faintly of biscuits). Borax was very fond of biscuits and he munched the prince down in one gulp. Knight Sir Trevor had missed the whole thing because he'd been in the kitchens cooking butterfly cakes. Burt arranged for the knight's head to be cut off with a big axe. Trevor wasn't happy about it, but agreed it was fair enough since he'd really messed up. He was allowed a last meal. He had butterfly cakes. (He said they were a bit dry and could have done with less time in the oven.)

Now let's get back to Castle Sideways. It's a lot like King Arthur's Camelot, but with a much sillier name. There's really only one important thing to remember about Castle Sideways and that's that Castle Sideways really is sideways.

Like all knights, Knight Sir Louis has a horse. His horse is a specially-made robot horse called Clunkalot. Clunkalot is Louis' faithful friend and also doubles up as sleeping quarters.

Clunkie isn't really afraid of anything. He once flew inside an ogre's stomach just to rescue a potted plant. It was a sunflower and he'd grown it from seed himself. He wasn't about to let some big, green oaf eat it.

Clunkie doesn't say much, or even neigh much. But he does compose poetry in his spare time, especially haiku. Here's one of his favourites:

Oh, my sunflower
Swallowed by a great, green brute.
That ogre is toast.

Clunkalot was built for Louis by the court wizard, Pearlin.

Young Pearlin isn't a fully qualified wizard yet. And she's not just a wizard. She's also an inventor. A sort of wizentor . . . or invizard.

WOTCHER
I'M MAGIC
I AM

Anyway, she comes from a big town down south called Larrrrrrndun. She came north to enter Master Mysto's Marvellous Mysterious and Mystical Academy of Magic and Magical Machines (called MMMMMMMM for short). Unfortunately, her scholarship was cancelled at the last minute. Why? Mysto had suddenly turned evil and run off into the woods. As a result, Pearlin is mostly self-taught.

Great. So now we've established some facts we can really get going.

CHAPTER 3

"And now on NewsKnight, a very special guest. We'll be interviewing champion of Castle Sideways, Knight Sir Louis . . ."

REPORTER: Louis, welcome to the studio.
SIR LOUIS: Thank you, Geoff.

REPORTER: My name's not Geoff.

SIR LOUIS: I know. I just thought I'd call you
Geoff.

REPORTER: Tell me, Louis. How old are
you?

SIR LOUIS: I'm twelve years old.

REPORTER: Really! And when did you
decide to become a knight?

SIR LOUIS: After breakfast.

REPORTER: I see. And your most death-
defying battle so far was . . . ?

SIR LOUIS: Probably when I had to unwobble
the wobbly tooth of Ogre Crumbletank. He
refused to go to the dentist.

REPORTER: I thought it would be the feud
with Fiery Fangsmasher the Purple
Dragon of Grizzlytum.

SIR LOUIS: That was easy. She had an itch she
couldn't scratch. She's actually quite nice.

REPORTER: Tell me, is there anything you
fear?

SIR LOUIS: Nothing.

REPORTER: I heard . . . wasps.

SIR LOUIS: No! I'm not afraid of wasps. Not one bit. There isn't a wasp here, is there?

REPORTER: Maybe there is, maybe there isn't . . .

SIR LOUIS: If there is, I might have to pop out. Not because I'm afraid or anything. Just because I might feel like going somewhere else.

REPORTER: I see. BUZZZZZZ!

SIR LOUIS: AHHHH!

REPORTER: You ARE afraid of wasps!

SIR LOUIS: No!

REPORTER: I don't believe you.

SIR LOUIS: Can I go now?

CHAPTER 4

My goodness! Chapter Three was almost as silly as Chapter One. Let's have a proper old-fashioned story for a bit.

Once upon a time there was a boy called Louis. He wished for all the world to follow in his father's footsteps and become a farmer. When he was old enough he would help his father, tending to the animals and crops. But very quickly, Louis' father realized his son was not meant to be a farmer. When Louis took the cows to pasture, they would not eat. When Louis took the cows for milking, they would not express. And when Louis

sowed seeds, the plants would not grow. So, one day his father told him that he was not to help in the fields any more. And this made Louis very sad. He wanted to impress his father, but how could he when everything he did turned to disaster?

The next day, Louis stayed with his mother, Trixie. She had errands to perform around the village. First, they ran to each of the four defence towers, pulled themselves up the rope ladders, looked about for any trouble and, seeing none, slid down the emergency poles. They stopped in at Nana's and helped her polish all her pots, pans and

other funny bits of metal until they gleamed. Then they went to the village hall where Trixie showed a group of villagers how to jump and stretch and roll. Louis joined in too. When they arrived home, Trixie and Louis took the carpets outside and beat them until they had banished every last mote of dust. Trixie showed Louis several different moves, including the lunge, the sideswipe and the surprise whack. As they worked they told each other jokes and stories and made each other laugh.

Louis planned to ask his father if he could work on the farm the next day. But when his father came home, Louis forgot to ask because he was so busy telling him all the things he had done that day with his mother.

The next morning, Louis helped his mother inspect the four towers again. Then his mother showed him how to hang out a washing line using

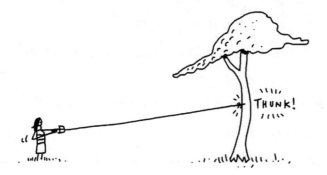

a bow and arrow. She fired with deadly accuracy at a tree, then pulled the line taut. Later, Louis had to use all his might to squeeze the wet washing through the ringer. He watched his mother squeeze the wet washing by hand. It seemed her hands were as strong as the ringer. All day long they told each other stories of brave knights and of derring-do. Louis planned once again to ask his father if he could work on the farm the following day. But when his father came home, Louis forgot. He spent all his time telling his father about the stories he'd heard.

The next morning his mother had to go to the big town for an important meeting. Louis stayed home to do the chores. She told him:

'Listen Poppet, do not answer the door to any strangers. Is that understood?'

But just after midday someone did knock at the door. Louis ignored it but the knock came again. He ignored it a second time, but the person knocked a third time.

'I say, what a marvellously clean carpet I spy

through the window!' said the person. 'Such fine work.'

Louis felt proud that someone had noticed his efforts. Louis forgot his mother's warning and answered the door. It was a door-to-door sales  witch carrying an old leather briefcase. The witch smiled a wide, false smile. Her eyes sparkled a sickly yellow like nuggets of sulphur.

'Can I interest you in some nasty tricks?' asked the witch.

'No, thank you,' replied Louis.

'I see. Well, is there any chance of a drink, young sir?' asked the witch.

'We have milk,' replied Louis.

'That will do nicely,' said the witch, 'though I have no money. You must have something in return.'

'Like what?' asked Louis.

'A way to impress your father perhaps?'

Louis gasped. Then the witch reached into her leather briefcase and produced a handful of seeds.

'These are magical seeds,' she whispered. 'Sow these and you'll have the biggest harvest you've ever seen!'

Louis held out his hands and the witch poured the seeds into his palm.

'But don't tell your father you've planted them or they won't grow,' she said. 'Just sow them in the ground and wait. He'll see what kind of farmer you've become!'

Then the witch drank down her milk, smiled a sly smile and strode away cackling.

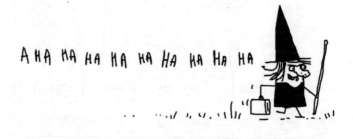

A HA HA HA HA HA HA HA HA HA

That night after his parents had gone to bed, Louis crept outside to plant the seeds. He was sure his father would soon be impressed.

The next morning Louis was woken by shouts and hollers. He ran downstairs. Father was in despair, pacing around Mother in the kitchen and tugging at his hair.

'They'll ruin us,' he said, pointing. 'Ruin us!'

Louis looked outside, astonished. The seeds had already grown into enormous plants. They stood twice as tall as the house, with thick rough stems. At their tops were two giant leaves with needle-like

teeth that snapped together like great mouths. The plants nearest the house were pulling their roots out of the ground and trying to walk.

'They'll eat all the crops,' moaned Father. 'And the cattle,' he whined. 'And then probably us!' he whimpered as he hid under the table.

'It's my fault,' said Louis, hanging his head. He explained the whole thing: the witch, the milk, the seeds. All done to impress his father. Louis expected his parents to be angry and punish him. Instead his father smiled weakly.

'The fact is, Louis, you're just not a farmer. You take after your mother. You're a warrior!'

Louis looked at his mother, Trixie. She smiled at him. He noticed that she seemed very calm despite all the man-eating plants trying to burst out of the soil. At that moment she was putting on her thickest leather apron. She reached up and took a small copper pot off the wall and put it on her head.

'My armour is still at Nana's after we polished it,' she said. 'But this'll do. Now . . . what shall I use as a sword?'

She grabbed a long metal fish slice.

Father explained, 'When your mother was a little older than you, she trained at Castle Sideways. You did know, right? That she's the village knight, our protector. And Chief of the local Guild of Knights!'

Louis shook his head. No! Now he wondered if that's where she'd gone the day before.

Trixie took the large lid from a jam pot and held it as a shield.

'Back in a jiffy,' she said.

And with that, she ran outside and straight into the man-eating plants. Louis watched open-mouthed as she barged and bashed and sliced her way through the evil plants. They snapped and writhed and tried to catch her but she was too fast. As it seemed she was about to win single-handed,

one plant behind her pulled its roots free. It reached down with green snapping jaws, ready to munch. Trixie might have been swallowed, apron, pots and all, had it not been for Louis who ran out of the house, picked up a bow and arrow and, with deadly accuracy, skewered the plant with the washing line.

From that day forward Louis vowed to become a knight like his mother. He became the finest knight in the land and the king's favourite. And they lived happily ever after . . .

Whoa there! Hang on! That sounds like the end. But it's not the end. This is just the end of Chapter Four. Goodbye. See you in Chapter Five.

CHAPTER 5

Hello. Welcome to Chapter Five. Chapter Five is a very short chapter.

CHAPTER 6

I promise you this will be a proper chapter. Let's head back to Castle Sideways.

King Burt was getting ready for bed when a messenger arrived. The messenger had ridden for ten days without stopping. Journeyed over mountainous mountains, hilly hills and daley dales. Crossed rapid rivers, lurid lakes and mushy marshes. Struggled against searing sandstorms,

whipping whirlwinds and blasting blizzards (and some blasting wizards). All this he had done to get to Castle Sideways to bring his message.

AT LAST, the messenger arrived. He stumbled, exhausted, to the king's chamber. AT LAST, he knelt before his King to deliver his message of great portent. AT LAST, he reached into his pouch to find the message, written on a scroll of parchment. It wasn't there. He had left it behind!

So he went back the way he had come, back into the blizzards, whirlwinds and sandstorms, sploshing through marshes, lakes and rivers and over dales, hills and yes, mountains too. Finally he arrived home where he realized he did have the scroll after all. It was just hidden at the bottom of his pouch, crumpled under his umbrella. So he turned around and, well, you get the idea, finally arrived back at the castle.

'What is it, messenger?' asked King Burt.

The messenger leant on one knee and said, 'I have travelled far, my king, to bring you this scroll.'

'You wally,' said the king. 'Why didn't you just send an email?!'

He pointed to his computer. He liked sending emails to his subjects. It meant he didn't have to go out and see them.

'I couldn't, my king. The internet has not yet been invented in the outlying regions. It's because we live in the past,' explained the messenger. It

32

was true. They lived about a hundred years before everyone else.

'Really?!' exclaimed the king. 'How awful!'

He unrolled the scroll and read the terrible news. What did it say? Well . . . you'll have to wait until the next chapter to find out. But the king read it and wasn't happy. He quaked to his toenails. Help was needed. Urgently.

'KNIGHT SIR LOUIS!' he shouted. 'COME AT ONCE!'

But nothing happened.

'Maybe send him an email?' said the messenger.

As luck would have it, Knight Sir Louis was nearby in the castle stables. More precisely, he was inside his robot horse, Clunkalot. Louis was downloading a brand new update from the wizentor Pearlin.

'What's the update for?' emailed Louis to Pearlin.

'It's a new language for Clunkalot,' emailed Pearlin. 'It's called Hee-Haw-Hee-Haw. Donkey language to you and me, right? So he'll know what donkeys are saying. Nice, yeah?'

'Brilliant,' wrote Louis. 'Very useful.' Though he wasn't sure it was.

Then the king's email arrived.

One second later, Clunkalot was running as hard as he could.

Ten seconds later, Knight Sir Louis was in the king's chamber, ready for his next mission.

CHAPTER 7

YE
MEDIEVAL
NEWS

Date: The Year of Our Llama 802. The Month of Turnip. Day the fifth and a quarter.

Hear ye! Hear ye! To all subjects of His not-very-voted-for Majesty King Burt the Not Bad, this news has just cometh in . . .

DAMSEL OF DISTRESSE

from ye correspondent Squire Typo.

Last Thors Day the peaceful Festival of Coin Counting in the mean old town of

Pennypinch was interrupted most sudden, by a-thumping and a-whacking.

When a-looking up, the residents spied an enormous Damsel, walking not only IN to the town, but also ON to it. Several dwellings were flattened when the enormous 'Damsel of Distresse' came a-romping through the high street, a-firing hot balls of blue fire from her horrible mouth.

One observer, a Mistress Sewersmell (12½), exclaimed, 'Cor blimey, she was tall as five houses with a pointy hat like a tower. Nothing could stop her and her big clanking shoes. She was dead rude and went straight for ye bank and nicked all our money. I did a-wailing for an hour, then I remembers I keep all me money in me knickers so I hadn't lost a penny. Ha!'

The enormous Damsel has also been seen in the villages of Cashlington, Sutton Goldfield and Much Firmlock. On each occasion she has stolen coins of gold, silver and chocolate.

Wizards have been studying her footprints and have concluded she is very big.

Concerned banker, Lord Pockets (97), was heard to say, 'This giant Damsel must be stopped or the kingdom will run out of money.'

Concerned tuck shop owner, Candy Underpants (32), added, 'What with this Damsel, chocolate coins is melting right out of the market.'

OTHER NEWS

In other news, tea has just been invented.

Louis looked up at King Burt who was trying his first cup of tea.

'This is terrible news, sire,' said Louis.

'I know,' said King Burt. 'We must not run out of chocolate!'

'Yes, Your Majesty,' said Louis, slightly worried the king hadn't noticed the main problem, 'or of gold and silver.'

'You must find this giant Damsel and stop it!' said the king.

'Yes, sire,' said Knight Sir Louis.

'And once you've stopped it . . . find out who sent the Damsel of Distresse and bring them here to our deepest, darkest dungeon!'

'Of course, sire.'

'And once you've done that you must find me some biscuits for this tea. It's delicious.'

Louis bowed, climbed onto Clunkalot and sped away to battle.

CHAPTER 8

Actually, he didn't speed away immediately. First of all he went to see Pearlin and asked for the following: a packet of glue powder and a set of bagpipes. Pearlin also fitted a new can-opening gadget for Clunkalot.

CHAPTER 9

It didn't take long for Louis to find the giant Damsel. He simply used Clunkalot's special sensors to detect the boom of her huge feet.

'There she is, Clunkie!' said Louis, peering into the distance as the Damsel clattered her way along the edge of a river.

'She's heading for that stone bridge,' he said. 'We'll cut her off there!'

Clunkie galloped as fast as he could, which was very fast, but not quite fast enough.

'We're not going to make it,' said Louis. 'Turn on Extra Feet!'

Good old Clunkalot did as he was asked and lowered four extra legs from his body. He doubled his speed.

WHOOSH!
KABAM!

They reached the stone bridge ahead of the Damsel, but only just. She looked angry. And very, very, very-very, very-very-very, yes another very, more very, even more very tall. Louis had to think fast. He needed a plan. It had to be clever and cunning and . . . aagh! . . . he just didn't have enough time. So, instead he shouted:

The Damsel stopped.

'Oh,' said Louis, surprised. 'I didn't think that was going to work.'

The Damsel lowered her head to look at the tiny specks that were Knight Sir Louis and Clunkalot. She smiled. Not a nice smile. It was the kind of smile somebody does if you've just stubbed your toe and they thought it was funny. Then she opened her mouth.

'Uh oh!' said Louis as her enormous tongue rolled out. He remembered what the newspaper had said about firing hot balls of blue fire from her mouth.

Blue like dragon fire! thought Louis, who'd seen a few fire-breathing dragons in his time (nice ones

who warmed up your dinner for you and not-so-nice ones who wanted to eat you for dinner).

The first ball of fire hit Louis' shield. The shield vaporized. The next ball hit his lance. Gone in an instant. Louis pulled his sword from its scabbard and clicked his heels into Clunkalot's side.

'CHARGE!' shouted Louis, and Clunkalot obeyed. A moment later a ball of blue fire hit the spot where they'd stood. The fireballs came thick and fast as they charged.

'If we get close, she won't dare fireball herself,' shouted Louis. 'Of course, we might be crushed by one of her giant shoes . . . Ha!'

Just then he looked up and saw the Damsel spit a blue fireball right at them.

I'm going to be frazzled! thought Louis. It was all rather frightening. But Louis found his most sensible ideas often appeared when he was under pressure.

A little voice in his head said, 'Use your magic sword, dummy!'

So he did. He raised it high in the air. The fireball hit the blade.

Guess what happened? Or don't. You can just carry on reading and find out.

CHAPTER 9.5

Now might be the right time to explain a little bit about Louis' sword. Here is an extract from an old diary.

The Month of Toadstools

Day the Second

At the wizentor's conference. Truly inspiring! Went to the sword making workshop today. Had no idea about all these amazing swords, like one made by some watery ladies in a lake, another one that glows when baddies are near and even one that can turn a little cat into a big green tiger. But I want to make something even better! Something fit for the greatest hero of our times.

Day the Third

Still at the conference. Went to fascinating workshop on ways to store dragon fire. Spoke to wizard chums about my sword idea. Most were supportive save for one young wizard called Barry or Harry or something. He laughed at me and said the future wasn't swords, but bazookas and potatoes. I told him he needed to get out more. Also that he should have a bath because he smelt dreadful. He stormed off muttering something like, 'I'll get my revenge one day, ha ha ha!'

Day the Fourth

Back home. Doing some research on swords. All famous swords have a name. Excalibur. Glamdring. Tizona. I will name mine . . . Senator Jibber Jabber Ticket Flick It Sprocket Wicket Dingle David! Or Dave for short.

Day the Ninth

Tried loads of different ways to make an awesome sword but so far all I've done is set fire to my bedroom.

Day the Eleventh

Seven of my cousins came over with a smashed magic mirror and asked if I'd like it. Gave me a brilliant idea! I'm going to forge a sword from the shards of the mirror. Wonder what will happen?

Day the Fourteenth

Senator Jibber Jabber Ticket Flick It Sprocket Wicket Dingle David is finished. I made him out of the magic mirror and now he's strong and shiny and full of magic. I think this could be a turning point in my career! Maybe I'll set up a school for wizards one day?

Also, I added a special feature to the sword. No one evil can touch it. It repels evil spells. I will test it on my nasty Aunt Fury next month at the family get together.

Day the Twentieth

Discovered a weird flaw in the design. Dave's edge is so sharp that when the wind whistles over the edge it slices the air into fragments. It sounds like a bunch of parrots being sat on by a rhinoceros. Ugh!

<u>Day the Twenty-first.</u>

Discovered an even weirder thing today. Turns out walruses like Dave's singing and they like it a lot.

Let's leave the diary there, shall we? The point is, Dave is a very tough, famous and (important bit) very shiny sword. Let's get back to the action and see what happens.

CHAPTER 9
(CONTINUED!)

The Damsel's fireball scorched down as Louis lifted Dave. The fireball crashed into the sword. It was fully expecting (and hoping in a nasty sort of way) to make Louis very hot and turn him into dust. So, the fireball was confused to find itself bouncing around inside a glass and silver prison. What on earth was going on?

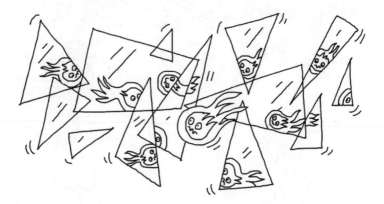

Well, what was going on was this: Dave had trapped the fireball using magical reflections. As long as he kept the fire bouncing around inside his shiny blade, it would be unable to cause any harm.

Louis swung Dave upwards, throwing the fireball back out the tip of the sword. The fireball was suddenly free and heading back the way it had come: towards the Damsel's mouth. The fireball didn't mind. It just wanted to blow something up and now, after all that frustrating bouncing around, it was going to get its chance!

The Damsel's tongue was frazzled!

Oh! All right then.

But that wasn't the end of the battle!

The Damsel spoke for the first time (with a smoking tongue).

'Prepare to be flattened,' she lisped.

'I don't think so,' said Louis.

'I mean it!'

'Actually, it's you that should prepare,' explained Louis, 'to be switched off.'

'What are you talking about?' barked the Damsel.

'I know you're not a proper, actual person,' said Louis. 'It's obvious you're some sort of devilish machine!'

'How dare you!' said the Damsel.

'I'll prove it,' said Louis.

'You won't!' said the Damsel and lifted her foot to crush Louis and Clunkalot. But Louis whipped out the bagpipes given to him by Pearlin.

'Ha! What are you going to do?' mocked the Damsel. 'Pipe me to death?'

Louis didn't reply. He simply blew very hard into the bagpipes. Jets of something like water flew out of the pipes and splattered over the Damsel.

'AH!' she screamed. 'I can't move! I CAN'T MOVE!'

'Of course not,' said Louis. 'I just splatted you with Pearlin's Mega Glue!'

The giant Damsel OF Distresse turned into the giant Damsel IN Distresse. She started to cry. Big blobs of engine oil fell from her eyes and splashed greasy streaks onto her giant pink tunic.

'Oh! I AM a machine!' she wailed. 'It's true!'
And then she shut down. Her arms fell limp.
Her eyes shut. Her wrenching, grinding gears fell
silent. She stood like an enormous statue, with a
message blinking on her forehead saying,

OIL FILL REQUIRED 🛢

60

'Let's find out what's inside this thing,' said Louis. 'Can-opener!'

Clunkalot trotted up to the Damsel and lifted a foot. Pearlin's new can-opener gadget flicked out and whizzed around. It cut a neat door-sized hole in the heel of the Damsel, just big enough for Knight Sir Louis.

'Thanks, Clunkie.' And Louis stepped inside.

Clunkalot thought this was an excellent time to write a new poem. Here's what he came up with:

Those who speak with fire
and hurl hot abuse... beware
when insults return.

CHAPTER 10

It was dark inside the robotic Damsel. Louis had to feel his way along, scraping his steel gauntlet on the iron walls. His hand touched a metal rung fixed into the wall and he started to climb. He went up and up until he found himself inside the robot's belly. A dim blue light lit a metal door with a round wheel handle. He tried to turn it but it wouldn't budge.

Whoever it was sounded nervous.

'Who are you?' asked Louis. 'Are you the driver of this machine?'

'Yesses!' said the voice. 'Er . . . No! Kind ofs! Maybe! A little bits!'

'That doesn't make sense!' said Louis.

'Go aways, please!'

'Unlock this door!' demanded Louis.

'What is you on abouts?' said the voice. 'This door ain't locked no more! Not since you knocked out the power.'

'Well, I can't open it!'

Louis watched as the wheel started to turn. It screeched metal against metal with each little twist.

'No,' said the voice. 'I suppose it just sticks a little. See!'

The door opened to reveal a hairy kind of pig-like creature, with hooves where hands might have been and a grey, wet snout where a nose might have been. Around its neck was an enormous ruff with little bells in the shape of acorns.

'There,' explained the creature, 'it weren't locked.'

Louis pointed his sword at the animal. 'Hold it right there!'

'Whoops,' it said, 'bit silly-billies of me.'

'Who . . . and what . . . are you?' asked Louis.

'I am Mr Catalogue,' said the creature.

'Mr Catty-Log?' said Louis unconvinced.

'Cat-a-log!' retorted the creature.

'You look like a pig.'

'How dares you. I is no pig. I is a boar. A wildish boar.'

Louis examined the creature. It was a boar, but it was also standing on its hind legs like a person.

'You don't look very wild,' said Louis. 'You look quite domesticated.'

This seemed to please Mr Catalogue very much.

'I tries. I tries,' it said, then sighed. 'Well, I suppose I'm under arrests. Fair enough. But I want a fair-ish trial, OK?'

CHAPTER 11

THE FAIR TRIAL OF MR CATALOGUE!

Mr Catalogue the boar came peacefully to Castle Sideways and the trial began the very next day. King Burt the Not Bad decided to have a day away from playing computer games so he could be judge. He really liked wearing the silly wig. As the accused was an animal, the jury was made up of twelve randomly selected mice.

'Tell us your story then,' said King Burt. 'It'd better be good or you'll find yourself in prison for the next million years!'

Mr Catalogue gulped and started the defence:

'Once upon a things, I was born. In the beginning I was just a-grunting and a-snorting and all happy with just being a boar. Then one days this metal man turns up. He is feeding me a fizzy potato and suddenly I is not thinking about acorns and truffles and other delicious munchies. Now I is also wonderings what life is about, and knowing things like the square roots of a nine is a three and that.'

'Sounds like magic,' said Pearlin to Louis.

'Could be,' said the boar, who'd overheard. 'Though having a bigger brain ain't all rainbows. I was more happy when I was just a boar snuffling for toadystools. Anyways, I is not liking this metal man because he has a whole bag of these potatoes and they is smelling of composts and eggs that's gone all pongy. He gives me some papers and on 'em is my new name and suddenly I'm reading for the first time and see I is now called Mr Catalogue. And this is special silly as I isn't even a Mister. I is a Misses.'

Knight Sir Louis and the rest of the crowd looked more closely at the boar. It . . . or rather she . . . certainly did have long and rather pretty eyelashes. (Mind you, so did King Burt.)

Mr Catalogue continued, 'These papers also show he got plans for me and I don't have no say in it. So I makes a run for it. But the metal man grabs me and draws a picture of some sausages and I get the hint, 'cause saussies is made of boars and piggywigs, unless they is them mushroomy ones.'

'Sounds very unfair,' said King Burt, who was

warming to Mr Catalogue. Louis agreed. This wasn't the sort of adversary he'd been expecting inside the giant Damsel.

'Next thing I know, I is in charge of this big metal damsel thing and I'm being sended off to steal monies. My job is to keep pedalling all the times. And I say, what if I refuse and the nasty

TRUNDLE ·
SQUEAK

metal man draws some burgers and I get the hints again. Though that don't make no sense, 'cause burgers is made of cows or sometimes sheepies but not piggywigs. Anyways, I do what I'm told. But I don't knows how to stop the Damsel shooting its fireballs and stamping on peoples. And I is thinking I'm in big troubles if someone ever finds me, and now they have and it's you lot.'

'This metal man,' said Louis, 'do you mean a knight? Like me?'

'Yeah. I suppose so. But much bigger,' said Mr Catalogue.

King Burt leant forward. 'And what did he look like? What was his name?'

'That's two questions I is answering with the same answer, your majestic wonder,' said the boar. 'The Stripy Knight!'

King Burt gasped, 'The Stripy Knight!'

'Yes, the Stripy Knight!'

Louis gasped as well, 'Not the Stripy Knight!'

'Yes,' said the boar again. 'The Stripy Knight!'

'Who's the Stripy Knight?' asked Pearlin.

'Haven't the faintest idea,' said Louis. 'Maybe we should ask the police?'

So they did.

CASTLE SIDEWAYS CONSTABULARY

FILE ID: 12345ONCEICAUGHTAFISHALIVE

DATE: YEAR OF OUR CHEESE WHEEL 798.
THE MONTH OF AVOCADO.
DAY THE TWENTY-TWELFTH.

CRIMINAL ALIAS: 'THE STRIPY KNIGHT'

REAL NAME: DUNNO

HEIGHT: BIGGISH

NOTABLE FEATURES: STRIPY ARMOUR

REPORT: The true identity of the criminal wot is known as the Stripy Knight is unbeknownst to us at this here-fore-to moment in time. We are unaware of his date of birth, his place of origin or his motives for being such an unpleasant pain in the rear behind.

He is currently the constabulary's most-wanted naughty man, being responsible for attacks on Castle Curly-Whirly, Castle Backwards and Castle Round-the-Twist. He is also wanted for the grand thievery of gold, silver and chocolate.

There is a reward for information leading to the arrest of said criminal which is: one bucket of finest manure.

CHAPTER 12

And now the verdict of the jury in the trial of
Mr Catalogue:

74

CHAPTER 13

Imagine for a moment that a whole day has passed since we last met Knight Sir Louis and Mr Catalogue the boar. Imagine that Mr Catalogue has been cleared of any naughtiness by the jury of twelve mice. Imagine that Louis and Mr Catalogue have talked and laughed and become good friends. I want you to do this because it is exactly what happened. Louis realized Mr Catalogue was not a bad sort of boar at all.

Unfortunately, all the stolen money had already been collected by the Stripy Knight.

HA HA HA HA
HA HA HA
HA HA HA
HA HA
HA

76

King Burt agreed with the jury that Mr Catalogue should go free. But because kings are very fond of money (and chocolate) he demanded that Mr Catalogue should help Louis on his mission.

'It's that or the dungeons,' said King Burt.

'Is a dungeon like a holiday with a jacuzzi and water slides?' asked Mr Catalogue.

The king showed Mr Catalogue round the dungeons.

'So, not a holiday park,' she realized. Mr Catalogue agreed to go with Louis.

'Where did the Stripy Knight go with the money?' asked Knight Sir Louis.

'Don't knows,' said Mr Catalogue. 'Only place I went was where the big Damsel-bot was made! Somewheres in the middle of a foresty-forest.'

'Then we'll go there and look for clues,' said Louis. 'How do we get there?'

'Never saw the way. The Stripy Knight used one of them blindfolds.'

'But he didn't cover up your nose?' asked Louis.

'No, that's true.'

'Do you think you'd recognize the forest from its smell?'

Mr Catalogue thought about it. 'I think so. It was a very chestnutty-smelling place for sure. And a bit of a stinkypoo of them toadystools that is all red with white spots which make you dead if you eats them.'

For a week and a day, Knight Sir Louis and Mr Catalogue searched the kingdom, riding here, there and everywhere on Clunkalot. When they arrived at a forest, Mr Catalogue put her snuffling, snorting snout to the ground and sniffed.

'Smells of acorns and apples!' said Mr Catalogue at the first wood. So, on they went.

'Smells of piney cones and parsley!' said Mr Catalogue at the second wood. So, on they went.

'Smells of lemon pips and cat moustaches!' said Mr Catalogue at the third wood.

'Cat moustaches?' said Louis, perplexed.

'Oh yeah,' said Mr Catalogue. 'They are right whiffy!' So, on they went.

Eventually they came to the most mysterious forest of them all. Dismal Wood. Once more, Mr Catalogue dismounted from Clunkalot. Once

more, she put her snout to the ground and sniffed. Once more, she said what she could smell.

'Smells chestnutty and of toadystools. We found it!'

'So what?' said a sly, croaky voice.

Louis looked down and there was the meanest, grubbiest-looking little man he'd ever seen. It was the wizard, Mysto!

CHAPTER 14

Mysto the dwarf was known as the world's greatest wizentor (and bestselling author of *Mysto. Mystery. My Story*). He used to be good until he decided it would be more fun to be bad. No one knew what had caused this dramatic change. He'd disappeared without trace a few years earlier.

There was a lot of nonsense said about Mysto. Some said he was five hundred years old with green skin, black eyes and a lot of nose hair. Some said he was a thousand years old with blue skin, yellow

MYSTO?

MYSTO?

MYSTO?

ears and a lot of nose hair. Others said Mysto was five gazillion years old with purple skin, nine eyes of different colours and a lot of nose hair. None of these people had ever met Mysto.

Louis and Mr Catalogue now saw that Mysto had light brown skin, jet-black hair and eyes of an unsettling amber colour. Though he did have a lot of nose hair.

'Mysto!' cried Knight Sir Louis. 'So you are the maker of the giant Damsel?'

'Of course,' boasted Mysto. 'No one else has the skills. No one!'

'But why? I hear, you used to be a good guy. What went wrong?'

'That's for me to know and you to cry into your pillow wondering about! HA HA!' said Mysto.

Although, in truth, Mysto couldn't really remember himself. That just made him even more grumpy and nasty.

'I don't think I'll be doing that,' said Louis.

'I think I'll just arrest you and take you in for questioning. We've searched a long time to find you.'

'And you'll have to search some more, too,' said Mysto mysteriously, 'for I am not really here!'

This confused Louis as it seemed Mysto was right in front of him. But then he noticed Mysto seemed to be hovering a few centimetres above the ground. And there was something a bit see-through about him.

'I'm just a hologram,' explained the dwarf. 'If you want to find me, you'll have to come into the deepest, darkest, most spooky part of the forest.

You'll have to take the PATH OF GLOOMY
DOOM! You'll have to avoid being eaten by the
grotipedes and stenchodiles. You'll have to find

a way through the unbreakable fence of ever-
growing oaks!'

'I'm not afraid,' said Louis, though he was a bit.

'You should be,' said Mysto. 'No one has ever
survived longer than a day inside Dismal Wood.'

'What about you?' said Louis.

'Well, obviously I have,' said Mysto.

'And there's the Stripy Knight and me,' said
Mr Catalogue.

'Yes, yes, you survived as well, but only because
I let you,' barked Mysto.

'And what about the one hundred and forty-five wigmakers who run the Dismal Wood Toupee Company?' remembered Louis.

'All right! All right!' said Mysto. 'Quite a lot of people survive inside the Dismal Wood, but that doesn't mean it's an easy life! For a start, there are all the wood wasps!'

Louis went as white as a sheet boiled in bleach (very white). His mouth went as dry as a bone that's been cooked at two hundred degrees for three hours (very dry).

'Wasps? Really? You're serious?'

'Yes,' said Mysto. 'Great big ones with horrible, shiny eyes and pointy, pokey stings for stabbing into knights!'

'So whats!' said Mr Catalogue. 'Knight Sir Louis ain't afraid of a buzzy old waspy. Are you?'

Louis quivered so much that his armour jangled. 'Afraid of wasps? Me? No way!' whimpered Louis.

He was glad his helmet was down so Mysto couldn't see him worrying. He tried to think of something brave to say: 'I eat wasps for breakfast.'

Mysto looked annoyed and said, 'Ugh! That's horrible. Well, you won't get any breakfast here  because they're all hibernating. Ha ha!'

Louis sighed with relief. Phew! No wasps.

'I challenge you,' said Louis, recovering. 'If I can find you in less than a day, will you answer one question truthfully? No tricks.'

Mysto's eyes narrowed to cruel, amber slits.

'Deal,' he said. 'But if you fail, I will send a nasty wizardy invention after you to cut off your heads!'

The hologram disappeared. Louis and Mr Catalogue jumped onto Clunkalot's back.

'Let's do this, Clunkie!'

Clunkalot reared up, neighed like an elephant (because he felt big and strong) and galloped towards the forest. The forest became thick and dark very quickly. Strange noises came from everywhere. Gurgles. Screeches. Rumbles.

Mr Catalogue looked around, worried, and asked, 'So is grotipedes and stenchodiles really real?'

'No,' said Louis, 'I don't think so.'

The path ahead of them petered out to nothing, covered in brambles and ferns. Then a huge, worm-like creature slithered down a tree towards them. It was bright yellow, with thick bristles. It had a huge wet mouth full of layers of teeth and it looked hungry.

'Then again,' said Louis, 'maybe they are real. Do you suppose that's a grotipede or a stenchodile?'

The creature was on the ground now and heading straight for them.

'I don't really care,' said Mr Catalogue.

'Good point,' said Louis. He turned Clunkalot around and raced out of the forest again shouting, 'If we survive this, we're going to need a new plan.'

WHOOSH

CHAPTER 15

Mysto the dwarf turned off his hologram machine and sat back on a tree stump to gloat. That silly knight would never find him.

The encounter left Mysto feeling very hungry, so he decided to make some soup. It was one of his mother's own recipes. Here it is:

MYSTOCHEF

MYSTOS' MUMMY'S MUSHROOM SOUP

FOUR HANDFULS OF MUSHROOMS
(NOT TOADSTOOLS-OR YOU'LL
GET THE TUMMY-SQUITTERS)
- ONE HANDFUL OF GREASE
- ONE FAT LEEK
- TWO BEAKERS OF GOAT'S MILK
- SALT OF THE SEA

THOU MUST FIRST CHOP UP THE MUSHROOMS
PROCEED TO FRY THEM IN GREASE WITH THE
FAT LEEK. WHEN THEY LOOK SOMEWHAT
BURNT, POUR THE IN THE MILK. LET IT
BUBBLE BUT NOT TOO HOTLY. AFTER AN
HOUR SERVE IT AND ADD SALT OF THE SEA.

It was a simple recipe, but good. As he was about to take his first sip he heard a voice.

'I'm here!' it said, and he spun around to see a metal horse, a boar with a ruff and a knight who bowed low.

CHAPTER 16

Welcome to Chapter Sixteen, where we take a sneaky look at a secret file!

SECRET FILE

TOP SECRET

SQUIRREL HELM SECRET SERVICE

SECRET FILE 783

REPORT PREPARED BY . . . well, it's a secret isn't it?

Many citizens have asked the question, how did Knight Sir Louis find his way to the hidden lair of Mysto? Only we at the SH Secret Service know the answer. Ha ha!

It turns out it is SO much easier to find secret lairs

hidden in forests by simply flying over the forest and looking down. (Add this amazing idea to the training file, please.) In this way you can see what's there without having to tramp through a whole forest. It also means you don't meet vile creatures like grotipedes or stenchodiles (see secret file 478 for more on these beasts).

Knight Sir Louis' horse, Clunkalot, is of course able to fly. And that is how Louis found Mysto's secret lair! P.S. Remember not to tell anyone. It's secret!

CHAPTER 17

Mysto almost fell into his mushroom soup when he saw Knight Sir Louis. No one had ever found their way to his secret camp. Others had visited, but only after being blindfolded and led through the forest. Mysto was impressed, but also suspicious. He looked from Louis to Mr Catalogue to the robot horse. He watched as Clunkie's wings folded back inside his body.

'Your horse is well made,' he said. 'I could have done better, of course. But still, not bad!'

Mysto tapped Clunkalot hard with his knuckles. Clunkalot didn't notice. He was still thinking about flying. He loved flying.

At that moment, Clunkalot was composing a new haiku in his robot-horsey brain.

It wasn't one of his best poems, but it shows just how much he likes flying. Anyway . . .

'We had a deal,' said Louis to Mysto. 'You promised to answer one question. Truthfully. No tricks. Where can I find the Stripy Knight?'

Mysto wrinkled his nose and let his eyes wander. He seemed to be searching around his filthy lair for something. He spotted whatever it was and smiled.

'I don't know his address,' said Mysto. 'But I do know how you can find it.'

Mysto pointed to some iron shoes. 'Those are my special time shoes. You can send your piggy friend here forward in time.'

Mr Catalogue looked a bit worried.

'Them shoes can take me into the futures?' she asked.

'Correct,' said Mysto. 'Go forward in this book to Chapter Twenty-Eight and you'll find the address of the Stripy Knight. Then come back and tell us what you've discovered.'

'Sounds well dangerous,' said Mr Catalogue.

'Yes,' replied Mysto. 'If you're not careful you'll go too far and end up in a different sort of book. Who knows where you'll be . . . *Twenty Thousand Leagues Under the Sea*? An encyclopedia of dinosaurs? A recipe book?'

Mysto smiled a nasty smile and Mr Catalogue gulped. Louis was suspicious.

'Wait,' said Louis to his friend. 'I'll go!'

'No!' insisted Mysto. 'You must stay here. The time shoes only work on animals with hooves!'

'I don't have hoofies,' said Mr Catalogue. 'I got trotters.'

'It works on trotters, too,' said Mysto, rather less convinced of himself.

Louis was sure Mysto was up to something. He looked at the time shoes. Then he remembered his sword, Dave. He knew that Mysto had made the sword long ago, when he was still good.

'Swear on Dave that you're not lying!' said Louis.

He pulled out his trusty sword and laid it on a stump. Mysto saw the sword and forgot everything

else. He'd not seen Dave for years and years. It was the finest thing he'd ever made. He suddenly wanted it back more than anything in the world.

'Who gave you that?' barked Mysto.

'It was a gift,' said Louis. 'From my mum. And she was given it by . . . well, it's a long story for another time.'

Mysto didn't care. He wanted the sword back. He reached out for Dave. He would cut down this knight and his silly boar. He grabbed the hilt of the sword. An instant later Mysto was flat on his back as though he'd been clonked on the head by a thunderbolt.

CHAPTER 18

'What happened to the grumbly man?' said Mr Catalogue. Mysto was still out cold.

'Dave knocked him out,' explained Louis. 'I forgot about his special features. It's all in the instruction manual.'

'Swordies have instruction wotsits?'

'Not normally,' said Louis. 'But Dave does.' And he pulled out a manual from inside his armour.

Congratulations! You have been gifted, have bought or perhaps inherited this genuine, magical sword. This sword, a steel 'WonderFighter' is the original masterwork of Mysto and has a pedigree name of Senator Jibber Jabber Ticket Flick It Sprocket Wicket Dingle David. It is customary to use the last name, so call this sword David or perhaps, Dave. Dave is a multifunctional, swishy-swashy, fighty machine, with a reflective index of one million winks.

Main Features:

1. This sword can cut things

2. This sword can slice things

3. This sword can chop things

Fashion Features:

4. This sword can be used as a mirror

Special Features:

5. This sword cannot be held by anyone evil and, in fact, it repels evil spells.

This feature was tested on Mysto's own evil Aunt Fury, who subsequently became lovely. She was still furious from time to time, but only about good causes.

The list went on, but Louis stopped at number five.

'Oo!' said Mr Catalogue. 'Evil spellies! Is that what's wrong with old grumbly-bumbly face?'

Mysto sat up and smiled. His amber eyes suddenly seemed friendly. 'Yes. Exactly,' said Mysto. 'But now I'm cured, thanks to you.'

He looked down at his hand. His palm was still wrapped around the hilt of the sword. He looked at Dave as though looking at a long-lost relative and sighed with happiness.

'Looks like new. Just as beautiful and sharp as the day I made him.'

'He's a great sword,' said Louis.

Mr Catalogue was still unsure whether to trust Mysto. But then he handed the sword back to Louis.

'I'm glad he's yours now,' said Mysto. 'And if I'm not mistaken, you're going to need him again very soon.'

CHAPTER 19

A day later Knight Sir Louis and Mr Catalogue had helped Mysto clear up his messy camp. In return he'd made them an extra-large batch of mushroom soup. The new Mysto was friendly, kind and cheery. He told jokes and sang songs and laughed often.

'It's time I told you about my curse,' said Mysto.

Knight Sir Louis was keen to hear the story.

'I was always a happy sort of fellow. Then one day I received some post, which was strange because the postman doesn't know where I live. It was a letter inviting me to the Wizentor of the Year Award. It was

being held in a place called Castle Boing. It said
I was going to win top prize for being the world's
best wizentor. I was flattered and packed my bags
immediately. When I arrived at Castle Boing there
was no one there. I thought perhaps everyone was
already inside waiting for me! And so I went in.
That was when the castle went pop and burst like
a balloon. And then I realized I was standing on
the edge of an enormous slide. Someone gave me a

shove and I slid wheeeeeee down and down under the earth and into a great pit. By the time I hit the ground I was very dizzy. And that's when I saw the most peculiar thing . . .'

'This potato didn't speak. He just handed me a note demanding I make the finest suit of armour ever. I told him I wouldn't. I'd been tricked and trapped. I was confident I could escape, but then I smelt something. Ugh! Horrible! Like old socks.'

'Ooo!' said Mr Catalogue. 'That's the same stinky pong I smelt when I was turned into a thinking boar!'

Mysto continued, 'The potato handed me another note saying if I didn't do as I was told, I'd be cursed.'

'And you still refused?' said Louis.

'Yes,' said Mysto. 'I wasn't worried. I always wear my anti-curse underwear. When you're in

my line of work, you have to protect yourself. I developed a set of underpants years ago that can repel most spells.'

'So what went wrong?' asked Louis.

'Well, because I was going to an awards ceremony I'd put on my fancy pants instead . . . the ones with gold braid and pictures of little unicorns. I had no way of defending myself. The evil curse hit me from behind, bazooka-strength!

WHAM BAM KAZAM ELIM FLAM

I was cursed and I became grumpy, irritable and generally horrible. Right up until just now when you saved me!'

Mysto continued, 'After the curse, I headed into Dismal Wood to set up an evil lair and make the armour. I made the hardest, toughest, smoothest suit of armour ever made. I used the finest purple steel and the hardest white diamond. I layered it up in stripes. That's why the wearer is better known as . . .'

Louis guessed, '. . . the Stripy Knight!'

'Hang on a mo,' said Mr Catalogue. 'Are you

sayin' that big old knight's just one
tiny potato inside?'

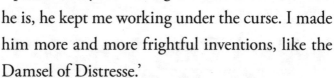

'I don't know what's inside now,'
said Mysto. 'Maybe a potato. Maybe
a person. Maybe nothing. Whatever
he is, he kept me working under the curse. I made
him more and more frightful inventions, like the
Damsel of Distresse.'

Knight Sir Louis nodded. It sounded like
the Stripy Knight had been up to all kinds of
tricks. Louis was pleased he'd frustrated the
Stripy Knight's plans, freeing Mr Catalogue and
now Mysto, too. But he remembered King Burt's
words:

'Find out who sent the Damsel of Distresse
and bring them here to be put into our deepest,
darkest dungeon!'

'Well,' said Louis, 'I'm glad you're feeling better
Mysto. I should probably say goodbye to you both,
head off and find this villain.'

'Hang on a mo!' said Mr Catalogue. 'King Burt
said I had to go with you.'

'You've helped me a lot already,' said Louis. 'You can go free now.'

'No ways,' said Mr Catalogue. 'You don't get to just jolly off on your own. We is a team now. If you is going, I'm coming too.'

Louis said, 'Are you sure you want to come along? It could be dangerous.'

'Danger is my middle name,' said Mr Catalogue.

'Really?' said Louis.

'No,' said Mr Catalogue. 'Don't have a first name, never mind a middle one. But if I did have a middle name it'd probably be Mildred 'cause I like that.'

'Me too,' said Louis.

'My middle name's unpronounceable,' said Mysto.

'I prefer Mildred,' said Mr Catalogue.

'No,' said Mysto, 'I mean my middle name is hard to pronounce. Thurgal-mountain-rengaroo-raa-bangle-twist-anoo-yoo-boo-targle-thang.'

'Still prefer Mildred,' said Mr Catalogue.

'Anywaaaaay,' said Louis, keen to head off on the next part of their quest. 'We need to find this Stripy Knight. Do these time shoes really work or was that some sort of trick?'

Mysto blushed and said, 'They do work, but yes, I was trying to trick you before. Do not go to Chapter Twenty-Eight under any circumstances.'

He looked at Mr Catalogue and continued, 'You need Chapter Twenty-Nine. That's where you'll find the Stripy Knight's address! Once you've found it, come straight back here. It might take you a few minutes, but to us it will seem like a single second!'

Mysto handed the time shoes to Mr Catalogue. She pulled them over her trotters. They felt heavy and tingled a bit.

'Right-o,' said Mr Catalogue. And without further ado, she stepped forward and disappeared into the future.

'Oh dear!' said Mysto.

'What's the matter?' said Louis.

'I didn't expect her to rush off like that! I hadn't told her how to come back in time!'

'Give me some time shoes too! I'll go after her,' said Louis.

The dwarf shook his head. 'Those are the only ones and besides, you don't have the right sort of feet!'

'We'll have to hope she works it out,' said Louis. Mr Catalogue was rather smart after all.

They stood around for a while hoping she might reappear from her time travels, but all remained quiet. Knight Sir Louis and Mysto exchanged a worried glance. They were both wondering the same thing: would they ever see Mr Catalogue again?

CHAPTER 20

Time Travel: The Future

You may wonder what it's like to travel into the future. There is no need to wonder. You are travelling into the future right now. And now. And now. You are always moving into the future. But *what if* you want to jump a long way into the future? The trick is to speed things up. That's where my time shoes come in. To travel into the future with the time shoes simply walk forwards. To go further into the future run faster. The faster you run, the faster time passes by. Simple!

But what if you want to stop travelling through time? That's easy too. Simply stand still and engage the time-lock clips. Once the clips are on you can walk around as normal without travelling through time.

WARNING: Do not dance in time shoes. Different parts of your body will end up in different times.

Imagine your head stuck in yesterday, your arms in tomorrow and your body left in today. Ouch!

Time Travel: The Past

Going into the past is tricky. In fact, it is almost impossible. But 'almost impossible' means 'slightly possible'. There are two things you must do.

Think how we travel into the past every day. We remember. Memories are from the past and our link to it. To travel into the past, you must remember things that have happened to you before.

The second thing you must do is to walk or run backwards.

CAUTION: Great care must be taken while running backwards! Falling over can cause sudden jolts in time travel leaving you who-knows-when!

When you arrive at the correct time simply use the time-lock clips again.

Have fun! And please use this invention responsibly!

CHAPTER 21

It was late. Knight Sir Louis and Mysto stayed up all evening waiting for their friend Mr Catalogue to return. She might come back at any time, like . . . NOW!

No!

Or NOW?

No!

Orrrrrr . . . NOOOOOWWWWW?

Still no.

But then at midnight . . .

. . .

Nothing happened.

CHAPTER 22

Mysto and Knight Sir Louis waited and waited for Mr Catalogue. Eventually they fell asleep. Then, at first light . . .

CLANK! Louis and Mysto leapt up, surprised. In front of them was a single time shoe. But there was no Mr Catalogue wearing it. The shoe smelt of hot mud and stinky eggs. Inside was some scrunched-up parchment.

Ho there, Nite Ser Looee and Mist-oh! It is Miz-turr Catty Log here from in the few-torr. I donut spel veree well, cuz I onlee hav trottors and no fingors. But heer go-erz anee way. I am a priz-nor in chaptor somfing and will need a rescoo wen yoo is getting hee-urr. In the meen time, heer is the addresse yoo waz wantin.

The address was on a neat, white envelope.

On the back was written something else, but it had been torn, perhaps during time travel. It simply read,

WATCH OUT FOR THE STINKY...

The rest was missing.

Louis was very relieved to discover Mr Catalogue was still alive. That was really good. It seemed she was a prisoner. That was bad. But he was a knight and it was his job to rescue people (and boars). So that was good again.

Brave Mr Catalogue had sent him the important

address. Louis was onto his enemy. He would go to Twisting Towers and capture the Stripy Knight. He would bring him back to Castle Sideways. Once again the kingdom would be safe. Hoorah!

Louis attached the single time shoe to his sword belt. Maybe it would come in handy one day?

Louis shook hands with Mysto and said farewell. Mysto gave Louis a squeezy 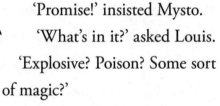 tube of something. He told him only to open it if he really needed it.

'Promise!' insisted Mysto.

'What's in it?' asked Louis.

'Explosive? Poison? Some sort of magic?'

'No,' said Mysto. 'Treacle.'

'Right,' said Louis. 'I see. I understand.' Though he didn't understand at all. He promised anyway, climbed inside Clunkalot and flew off towards Chapter Twenty-Three.

CHAPTER 23

Close your eyes. Actually, don't do that or you won't be able to read this. Imagine you've closed your eyes. Now imagine it's hot. You're in a wide, golden desert. The wind blows over the tall dunes. Now imagine you have left the desert behind and you're in the mountains. They rise up like giant, red shark's teeth, jutting out of the lush green pastures. Now imagine night has fallen across a smooth purple sea, sparkling with the reflections of a million stars. See all that? Yes? Wow, you've got a great imagination!

Knight Sir Louis saw all these lands from his window as he flew over the world with Clunkalot. He looked down below as they flew over the coast and over the strange green land of Verdig.

SWOOSH

Clunkie loved flying, of course. The air zipped up his nickel nostrils and whipped around his aluminium ears. He buzzed over clouds and waved a hoof at a passing flock of migrating geese. The geese were surprised to find a horse in the air. They all agreed later it was probably just a funny-shaped cloud.

As the moon rose, lighting up the clouds like silver foam, Clunkalot decided to do a loop-the-loop out of pure joy. But as he raced upwards, he felt something inside him go SPROING! After that, he felt another unpleasant feeling that was more like FUDURRRR! And last, but not least, he felt a very odd churning that went TSSSSSS-CK!

Knight Sir Louis was reading in his bed inside Clunkie, and also heard the strange noises. The flight computer started flashing.

PANIC STATIONS ARE LIKE
TOTALLY GO! I MEAN BIG,
BIG AGH! PANIC NOW!

Clunkalot was about to shut down and stop

126

flying. This was not good news as the ground was about a mile beneath them.

Clunkie's last thought before he fainted was, *What's that funny blue sparkle on the ground? Maybe I could write a poem about—* After that, he closed his iron eyelids and started to plummet directly downwards!

Knight Sir Louis was not frightened.

OK, he was a little bit.

I would be!

But Pearlin, the creator of Clunkalot, had planned for a malfunction just like this and had shown Louis what to do.

CHAPTER 24

TIME: Six months earlier.

LOCATION: Castle Sideways.

MORE PRECISE LOCATION: Pearlin's wizentor laboratory.

EVEN MORE PRECISE LOCATION: Near the window.

ALRIGHT KSL!

HI PEARLIN

NOW LISTEN UP!
I'VE MADE SOME SWEET
MODIFICATIONS
ON CLUNKIE,
YEAH?

WOW!
ARE THOSE WINGS?

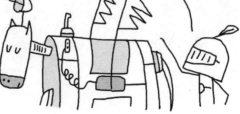

YEAH. CLUNKIE'S
A FLYER NOW!
WINGS. RUDDER.
BOOSTER.

CAN I DO A TEST
FLIGHT?

YEAH! BUT FIRST YOU GOTTA KNOW
THE EMERGENCY PROCEDURE
RIGHT. SEE THESE TWO ROWING OARS.

...ALL YOU DO IS ROW FOR YOUR LIFE. LITERALLY. HA! THE OARS MAKE THE WINGS FLAP FLAPPY FLAP. JUST KEEP IT FLAPPING LONG ENOUGH TILL YOU HIT THE GROUND.

ANYWAY, PROBABLY WON'T HAPPEN.

CHAPTER 25

TIME: Now.

LOCATION: Up in the air, but heading downwards.

Knight Sir Louis and Clunkalot were heading straight down towards the Verdig wastelands. AAGH!

Long ago, Verdig had been marshlands, wet and lush and full of strangler figs that curled and twisted around plump trees. Everything had been green. Green leaves. Green moss.

Green water. But that was ages ago: a thousand years, or maybe just a hundred, or perhaps just last Wednesday. Who knows?! But it dried up and everything crumbled and turned to tiny little grains, like sand, except they'd stayed green.

Louis heaved hard on the emergency oars. Each pull of the oars made Clunkie's wings flap. It was hard work. Louis could feel himself getting tired. But he didn't stop.

Finally, Clunkalot crash-landed on the ground. When he hit the green sands he fell onto his side and span around. Louis felt like he was inside a tornado. At last, Clunkalot slid to a stop.

Louis climbed out, bruised and shaken. He didn't care about himself though. He was worried about his trusty horse. He tried to restart Clunkie's computer. He whispered in the horse's ear. He spoke some magic words Pearlin had taught him. But Clunkalot didn't respond. Knight Sir Louis sat with his horse for a long while wondering what to do.

Normally Louis could work out how to save

the day. Plans would pop into his head and he'd go, *Oh yes, now I can fix things.* But right now, his brain was filled with other thoughts. Thoughts like: *Oh Clunkie! Please don't be broken! I feel so lonely now. I wish I knew more about magic and machines and being a wizentor.*

But, of course, we can't be good at everything. And in the end Louis was faced with a very difficult decision. He could give up his quest and go home. Or he could carry on alone.

He carefully folded Clunkie's legs under

his body, then covered him with a camouflage blanket to keep him hidden.

'Don't worry, Clunkie,' he said out loud, 'I'll be back with Pearlin to get you going again.'

He knew his horse probably couldn't hear him, but he wanted to say it all the same. The truth was, he was worried. Very worried. He was worried that Clunkie might never start up again. What if Pearlin couldn't fix him? Louis put his arms around Clunkie's neck and whispered sadly:

'I have to keep my promise to King Burt and capture the Stripy Knight. I'll be back as soon as I can.'

He was very sad to leave. He turned and started the long walk to Chewing Grunderpips. Louis' only comfort was that Clunkie would be safe here. No one would find his horse in this empty green wilderness.

But an hour later, the wind carried the sound of footsteps crunching through the sand. Someone was walking to the exact spot where Clunkie lay. If Clunkalot had been able to sniff, he would have sniffed a stench of hot mud and rotten eggs. If he had been able to see he would have seen a silhouette of a person with a two-pointed hat. The mystery person found the camouflage blanket and rubbed his hands.

'At last,' he said. 'My terrible plans have worked. Clunkalot is mine and soon Knight Sir Louis will also be at my mercy. No one suspects me. No one even knows who I am yet. Including YOU, reader! HA HA HA HA HA!'

CHAPTER 26

Knight Sir Louis walked for a long while. He tried not to think about Clunkie. He had to resist the urge to go back. But what could he do? He was good at fighting dragons, not at repairing magical machines. He walked until the sun came up. The sun saw Louis and wondered if it might be able to cheer him up. But no amount of shining seemed to help. So, the sun decided to give the rest of the day a miss. It ducked back under the horizon. A second night carried straight on from where the last one left off. Louis didn't mind because he was really tired and needed a good night's sleep. He stuck his sword, Dave, in the sand and lay down beside it. Louis looked up at the stars. The constellation of the famous flying horse Pegalot

was right above him. He sighed. It made him miss Clunkie all the more.

It wasn't easy to fall asleep. The moon decided (because the sun wasn't coming out) it should shine more brightly. Louis had to wait until a black cloud moved in front of the moon's shining face. Just as Louis was dropping off it started to rain and the pitter-patter on his armour was like a billion tiny steel drums playing a tune. Aagh! Eventually the rain petered out, but then the wind picked up. It whistled over the edge of his sword. Oh, no! Dave was singing. Before Louis could stand up and sheath his sword, a whole flopping, slapping, waddling pod of walruses crowded around. They'd come to listen to the dreadful singing of the sword.

'Isn't it simply marvellous?' said one walrus, in walrus language.

'Exquisite music,' said another.

'A masterpiece of harmony and melody,' said a third.

Of course, Louis didn't speak walrus so all he heard was:

BARRRR HUUURRRRK HOOOORL

He realized he wasn't going to get any sleep, so he stood up wearily, grabbed Dave and trotted off as fast as he could.

'How rude,' said the first walrus. 'I was enjoying that!'

Louis kept walking until he simply fell to the ground exhausted. At last, he slept. He slept until the sun decided it couldn't delay any longer and really should throw some light around the place.

Z Z Z Z Z Z Z Z Z Z Z Z Z Z Z Z Z Z Z Z Z Z Z Z Z Z

141

THESE ARE WORMHOLE WALRUSES, ABLE TO MAGICALLY TRANSPORT THEMSELVES WHEREVER THEY'D MOST LIKE TO BE.

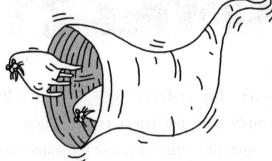

DOES THAT MAKE SENSE?

NO.

BUT CAN WE AT LEAST GET ON WITH THE STORY?

ALRIGHT. I SUPPOSE.

CHAPTER 27

Chapter Twenty-Seven was nervous. It was perilously close to Chapter Twenty-Eight.

Knight Sir Louis didn't like the sounds coming from Chapter Twenty-Eight. He decided it was sensible to skip it and go straight to Chapter Twenty-Nine.

DANGER

CHAPTER 28

AAAHHHHH!
BUZZZZZZ!
OOOOOOOO!
HELP!

CHAPTER 29

Knight Sir Louis was pleased to have avoided Chapter Twenty-Eight. It was a very unpleasant chapter. It sounded like a bunch of wasps up to no good.

Louis walked for a long while and at last stood in the town of Chewing Grunderpips upon the river of Pongeepoo. More precisely he stood in front of a huge block of flats called Twisting Towers – home of the Stripy Knight.

Knight Sir Louis thought of Clunkalot and Mr Catalogue. He decided it was time to stop feeling sorry for himself. It was now time to be brave and save the day! He approached the stairwell and prepared for battle.

He moved steadily and calmly. He was careful

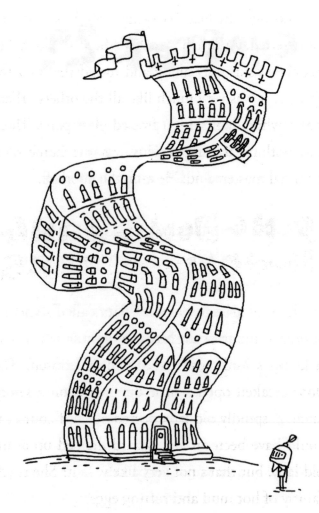

as he turned each corner of the stairwell in case someone was waiting for him. He passed the first floor, the second, the third, the fourth . . . he met no one. In fact, Twisting Towers seemed to be deserted. At last he reached the fifth floor. He marched cautiously along and found the door for Flat 56. It was very much like all the others. There was a white door with a frosted glass pane. There was nothing to suggest this was the home of a criminal mastermind! He rang the doorbell.

DING DONG DANG DONG DING DANG

He waited a little while and saw someone approach the frosted glass door very slowly. Louis held his sword steady and readied himself. The door creaked open a little bit. It was on a safety latch. A spindly old lady peered out. Of course, it could have been an evil wizard dressed up as an old lady, but that's not very likely. Is it? She smelt faintly of hot mud and rotting eggs.

'What is it, young man? Have you come about the boiler?'

'Er . . . no!' said Louis. 'Excuse me, does the Stripy Knight live here?'

'You want next door, deary,' said the old lady. Louis checked the address again. She was right. He didn't want Flat 56. He wanted Flat 58.

'Sorry!' said Louis, but the old lady had already closed the door.

Louis walked to Flat 58 and prepared himself again. He pressed the doorbell. It went:

WOOHAHAHAHAHAWOOHA HAWOOHAHA

The door creaked open to reveal . . .

. . . nothing.

Nothing at all. Not even a corridor. Just dark space. Knight Sir Louis didn't like it, but that was a good sign. That meant he'd come to the right place. He shrugged and walked carefully into the emptiness of Flat 58.

CHAPTER 30

As soon as Knight Sir Louis stepped into the flat, he fell.

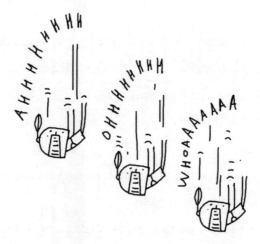

Then he stopped for a bit because shouting was making his throat sore.

'Wow, this really is a very long way to fall!' he said to no one in particular. Then because there was nothing else to do, he started shouting again.

'YAAAAAAAAAAAAA,' said Louis until, at last, he landed in something pulpy and squelchy.

'OOF!'

He sniffed. He'd landed in a darkish pit. The only light came from a few weak lamps hanging around the edges.

I must be a long, long way underground, thought Louis.

The pit smelt like soil and raw vegetables. He picked himself up and looked around. He spotted some kind of wall on one side of the pit. He walked over to it and touched it. Then he sniffed it.

Smells like potato! thought Louis. *But look at the size of it. It must be massive!*

It was indeed an extremely large potato, buried far underground. Carved in the side were two grand doors.

'I wonder . . .' he said, and pulled at the handles. The doors opened easily. He stepped inside. On the other side was an huge, evil lair fit for any evil knight. Everything had been carved out of the raw potato and it had been designed to look like a horrible, dark dungeon.

'AT LAST!' rang out a voice. 'KNIGHT SIR LOUIS IN MY DUNGEON!'

And then there was some mad laughter.

Louis looked around but couldn't see anyone in the dim lair.

'AT LAST! WE MEET!'

'Well, not really,' said Louis, looking around.

'THE GOOD KNIGHT AND THE BAD KNIGHT.'

'Excuse me!' Louis tried again, but the voice didn't care.

'THE NOBLE KNIGHT AND THE—'

'AHEM!' said Louis for a third time.

'OH, WHAT IS IT?' said the voice, annoyed.

'Why are you shouting?' asked Louis.

'It's for effect, isn't it?' explained the voice. 'To show you I'm dangerous and bad-tempered.'

'Oh, I see. Well do you mind not doing it, it's quite annoying.'

'Very well,' said the voice. 'As long as I can still laugh madly at the end.'

'Fine,' said Louis.

'Now where was I?'

'Wait a moment,' interrupted Louis again.

'Now what?' asked the voice, sounding quite peeved.

'Where are you exactly?'

'Isn't it obvious?'

'Not really. It's very dark in here.'

'Oh yes,' it said. 'I forgot the lights!'

Suddenly two bright spotlights clanked on. They shone beams of white light onto a throne. Sitting on it was . . .

CHAPTER 31

Knight Sir Louis strode up to the Stripy Knight. Up close, Louis could see how gigantic he really was. He was very tall, very broad and very stripy. Surely, whoever was inside must be enormous (and with enormous muscles). But Louis knew his job and he had his trusty sword, Dave, at his side.

'Mr Stripy Knight, you are under arrest by order of His Majesty King Burt the Not Bad.'

The Stripy Knight's helmet was down so Louis couldn't see his face, but the voice rang out as before, 'QUIET! I haven't finished gloating!'

'Whatever . . . get on with it though,' said Louis. 'I don't have all day.'

Louis had the strangest feeling the voice wasn't coming from the Stripy Knight at all. But who could tell in this strange lair with squashy walls?

'Erm . . . where was I?' said the voice, thinking aloud. 'At last we meet . . . blah blah. Good Knight, Bad Knight. Blah blah. Oh yes! THE LOSING KNIGHT AND THE WINNING KNIGHT!'

'Are you the losing knight?' asked Louis.

'Of course not!' said the voice, really quite annoyed now. 'That's you! You've lost!'

'But we've not had a sword fight yet!'

Louis drew his sword. 'Come quietly . . . or it's sword-fight time!'

'Oh, I will be going to Castle Sideways,' said the voice, 'but not as a prisoner. I will be going as conqueror!'

At that, Louis bounded forward and brought

his sword up to attack. He fully expected the Stripy Knight to fight back. But Louis swung his sword and immediately sliced the Stripy Knight's head right off. The Stripy Knight collapsed to the ground. It was over! Just like that. He had defeated

his foe easily. This was all very good, but it had
been a real let-down in the excitement stakes.

Knight Sir Louis noticed the Stripy Knight's
visor had flopped open. He got a look at the real
culprit behind the mask. It was . . . yes . . . just as
Mysto had said . . . a potato.

CHAPTER 32

Knight Sir Louis scratched his head. The Stripy Knight was in fact just a bunch of potatoes strung together. That didn't make sense! What was it with all this potato stuff? What on earth was going on?

'What on earth is going on?' said Louis.

Once again, he heard laughter, 'HA HA! FOOLED YOU!'

Now he knew the voice wasn't coming from the Stripy Knight. He heard footsteps.

CLOMP
CLOMP
CLOMP

Someone approached from the shadows. Before Louis saw him, he smelt him. The smell was of hot mud and rotting eggs. It turned his stomach. Ugh. Where had he smelt that before?

Had he caught a whiff of it in the desert when he'd left poor Clunkalot under the tarpaulin? He'd definitely smelt it when the single time shoe had come back from brave Mr Catalogue. He'd also smelt it at Flat 56 just before he'd fallen into this evil lair.

The person stepped into the light.

CHAPTER 33

'You didn't really think the Stripy Knight was the brains behind this outfit, did you?' said the wizard.

'Well, I did actually,' admitted Louis. 'Because everyone's heard of the Stripy Knight. But no one's heard of . . . whoever you are.'

'BAZOOKA HARRY!' shouted Bazooka Harry, for that was the evil wizard's name.

Bazooka Harry was exceptionally tall. Except he wasn't. He just wore a tall hat that made him a little bit taller than most other people. It was like a normal wizard's hat, except split in two so that it had two points. The hat smelt of old potatoes, because that's what it was made from. He wore fake ears over his real ones to make them look pointy and interesting. He had three arms, one on his left and two on his right. Though one of his right arms was invisible.

But he definitely had an evil moustache! That's like a normal moustache but longer and more pointed. And slung across his back was a magical bazooka. He used it instead of a normal wizard's staff. It could fire big, walloping magicking spells.

'Bazooka Harry?' said Louis. 'Never heard of you.'

Bazooka Harry laughed with a nasty hissing sound, 'HSSSSSS HSSSSSS HSSSSSS.' It was a very unpleasant way of laughing.

'No. I've been keeping myself to myself while the Stripy Knight did my dirty work. But soon everyone *will* know me. I don't work for the Stripy Knight you see. He works for me! He's my creation. I am the real villain here.'

And he smiled with his thin lips to reveal some very unpleasant, yellow teeth.

Some knights might have panicked at this surprising news. Here was a baddy even more bad

168

than the Stripy Knight. But Louis remained quite calm.

'Fair enough,' said Louis. 'Then I'll arrest you instead. One question though. Why is the Stripy Knight and this whole lair made from potato?'

'Hssss,' laughed Bazooka. 'Why? You fool! Because potato magic is the greatest of all magics.'

'Potato magic?' queried Louis.

'Oo, yes. The potato is the greatest source of the most naughty and terrible magic ever!'

'Are you sure?' asked Louis. 'Sounds silly.'

'Yes, I'm sure. Definitely. Er . . . I think so,' said Bazooka, a little less confidently than before. 'I'm sure that's what my evil mentor, Acidic Alan, told me. It definitely wasn't parsnips as they are a most sweet and disappointing vegetable. GAH! I HATE PARSNIPS!'

Louis actually agreed with this, but wasn't about to tell Bazooka that.

ACIDIC ALAN

'Anyway,' said Bazooka, 'the Stripy Knight is just a string of potatoes enchanted to appear alive. Impressive, no?'

'Hmm,' said Louis, who wasn't sure it was.

'It's not easy you know!' barked Bazooka.

'But WHY are you doing all this?' asked Louis.

He knew bad guys couldn't resist this question.

But would Bazooka Harry fall for it?
Maybe Bazooka Harry was different after all.

No, Bazooka Harry was no different.

CHAPTER 34

'I intend to take over Castle Sideways and become the new king!' explained Bazooka Harry. 'But I always knew it would be tricky to take the castle while its champion was defending it, even with a magical bazooka at my side!'

'You mean . . . ?' said Louis.

'Yes!' said the wizard. 'You. Champion knight of Castle Sideways. The famous Knight Sir Louis. I tried to think of ways to capture you and bring you here to my lair! But then I thought of a plan. A wonderful, horrible plan. Why not simply get you to bring yourself here? Lure you with rumours of an evil Stripy Knight, with the promise of an epic sword fight, with the promise of heroism and daring! What champion could resist? And it worked! IT WORKED! Hssssss! Now you are here and captured, and I can go to Castle Sideways and take over as king!'

For a moment Louis felt foolish. He had fallen right into Bazooka Harry's trap. He'd also lost Clunkalot and Mr Catalogue along the way. Maybe he didn't deserve to be champion knight after all? But then he remembered some of his mother's wise words. Only last week, she'd sent him a novelty mug with the words:

'When life knocks you down, the only thing left to do is to stand back up and bash life very hard on the head.'

Thanks, Mum, thought Louis.

Then he lifted his sword and said, 'Enough of this. I've decided I'm not captured after all. Prepare to do battle!'

Bazooka Harry nodded sagely and said, 'Of course, your sword, the mighty Senator Jibber Jabber Ticket Flick It Sprocket Wicket Dingle David, better known as Dave for short! Oh, I have a plan for this moment too. This is where I give you a terrible choice.'

The wizard aimed his magical bazooka at a wall and fired off a spell. The wall disappeared to reveal prison bars. Behind the bars sat a familiar hairy figure. It was Mr Catalogue. She looked very

 sorry for herself. She glanced up, surprised the wall had vanished.

'What's going on heres?' she said, then noticed Louis and jumped up to the bars with a big smile. 'Hoorays! I've been here ages and stuff. I needs rescuing, Louis, like a beautiful lady in a tower. But with more hair and bristles.'

'Good to see you, Mr Catalogue!' said Louis, meaning it. 'I'll have you out of there in just a second!'

'Afraid not,' said Bazooka Harry, pointing the bazooka at the boar.

He turned to Louis and said, 'Option one. You hand over your sword and join Mr Catalogue in my prison.'

'Nope,' said Louis.

'You haven't heard option two yet,' said Bazooka Harry, 'which is simple. Option two is I fire my bazooka again and turn Mr Catalogue into a rissole!'

There was a long pause. Expectation hung in the air like a giant question mark made of ticking alarm clocks.

Then Louis said, 'What's a rissole?'

'What do you mean "what's a rissole?"' said Bazooka irritably.

'I mean I've never heard of one. Is it some kind of instrument?'

'NO! It's a meat-based food product. Kind of roundish.'

'Like a meatball?' asked Mr Catalogue.

'Yes,' said Bazooka Harry, nodding, 'exactly.

You can mix in a bit of apple as well if you like.'

'No thanks,' said Mr Catalogue.

'Right, a meatball,' said Louis. 'Maybe in the future you can just say meatball instead of rissole?'

'Just make your choice,' said Bazooka sharply. 'Prison with Mr Catalogue or Mr Catalogue meatballs?'

Knight Sir Louis looked around. Could he leap and stop Bazooka Harry's spell before he cast it? No. The bazooka would be too fast!

Louis made his choice. Dave the sword clattered to the ground.

CLANG!

'No!' said Mr Catalogue.

'Yes,' said Louis. 'I won't see you turned into supper.'

And so, Bazooka Harry started laughing, 'HSSSSSSS HSSSSSSS HSSSSSSS HSSSSSSS HSSSSSSS HSSSSSSS HSSSSSSS HSSSSSSS HSSSSSSS HSSSSSSS HSSSSSSS HSSSSSSS HSSSSSSS HSSSSSSS HSSSSSSS HSSSSSSS HSSSSSSS HSSSSSSS HSSSSSSS HSSSSSSS.'

Basically, he went on laughing his sinister, hissy laugh for ages. If we wrote it all down here it would fill the rest of the book, so let's move on.

CHAPTER 35

A short while later, Knight Sir Louis was locked up with Mr Catalogue in Bazooka Harry's prison cell. Bazooka was gloating on the other side of the bars. He had beaten Knight Sir Louis with cunning. Louis hoped Bazooka might pick up Dave and be knocked out by the anti-evil spell.

'At last!' said Bazooka. 'The time has come to take control of Castle Sideways.'

Bazooka spoke magical words to the Stripy Knight who picked up his head and put it back on. The knight also grabbed Dave. The sword's spell had no effect as he wasn't truly alive.

Knight Sir Louis tried to stay confident.

'We'll break out of here and stop you,' he said, 'long before you reach Castle Sideways!'

'No, no, no,' said Bazooka with a horrible smile, 'because we'll be there oh so soon. We have the fastest horse in the kingdom.'

He pointed to another part of the lair. A hatch fell back and a horse strolled out.

'NO!' shouted Louis.

It was Clunkalot! Except his eyes glowed a horrible red. Clunkie had been repaired, but also changed. He gnashed his metal teeth and blew hot steam from his nostrils.

'WHAT HAVE YOU DONE TO HIM?'

'Just a bit of rewiring,' leered the wizard. 'Also I renamed him . . . STOMPALOT!'

It was true. Bazooka Harry had been behind Clunkalot's malfunction all along . . .

Bazooka Harry stepped into Stompalot's belly while his Stripy Knight climbed onto the horse's back. Stompalot unfolded his wings, took off and flew out of the double doors. They were heading away to conquer Castle Sideways and there was nothing Louis could do to stop it.

CHAPTER 36

Things were pretty bad for Knight Sir Louis. Really bad. Really, very bad. Really, enormously baddy-bad-bad.

Now, let's all just chill out for a moment and try and relax. Think of . . . soft things, like fluffy cushions, or the way a smooth banister feels under your palm. Or about cute things like purring kittens, or soft doggy tummies.

OK. Feeling calmer? Good. Let's get back to the action.

CHAPTER 37

Knight Sir Louis and Mr Catalogue sat on potato sacks inside their prison cell.

'It's all my fault yous is here,' said Mr Catalogue, upset. 'I should never have got meself captured. I almost got aways using the timey shoes, but then old Bazooka Harry clunked me on the head with a big potato and I went all dizzies. Now we're trapped forever and Bazooka has gone and won.'

'Not yet,' said Louis. 'We may be trapped in a magical prison deep underground but we're still alive! All we need is a really great plan.'

And that is precisely what Knight Sir Louis came up with.

Hi there! I'm Merry Pickle the Minstrel! And this is my new song. It's dedicated to Knight Sir Louis and Mr Catalogue in honour of their amazing escape from potato prison. It's my way of saying to them 'you are ace' though hardly anyone says 'ace' these days, which is a shame.

Knight Sir Louis.
Knight Sir Louis.
He's a hero.
Oh it's truey!

Now here's what happened in the wizard's jail:
the boar and the knight were turning pale.
With no food or fire, they began to quail.
Our champion Louis was about to fail.

The bars of the prison were thick and strong.
Could have caged a thing like big King Kong.
Oh, they were trapped, for their whole life long,
till the boar sniffed the bars:
'Hey, I knows that pong!

'These bars do whiff o' potatoes a bit.'
'Of course,' said Louis. 'I'm such a twit!
I'll get us out in a lickety-split.'
And out he pulled his survival kit.

Yes! The bars were made of potato-oh!
The bars were made of potato-whoa!
The bars were magical potato-yo!
And 'tater can be cooked, ho-ho!

The survival kit had pots and pans
and a camping stove with turbofans.

He boiled some water, made some steam,
oh, what on earth was Louis' scheme?

The jail bars soaked up the steam in a flash,
And turned the potato poles to mash.

'SNOORAY!' said the boar from her sniffy snout,
and they chomped
and they chewed
their way OUT-OUT!

CHAPTER 38

Did you enjoy the song? It's still a favourite across the land. It's also traditional to end by eating a large portion of mashed potato.

After Louis and Mr Catalogue escaped their potato prison, they had a good look around Bazooka's lair for anything useful.

They found one of Mr Catalogue's time shoes under a pile of potato sacks. The other shoe, if you remember, was still hanging from Louis' sword belt.

'I could use 'em and go back and save ourselves,' said Mr Catalogue.

'No,' said Louis. 'We don't know how long this cave's been here. We don't want you walking back into solid rock.'

'Ugh, good point,' said Mr Catalogue.

They decided to cut some very long ladders out of the huge potato. But then Louis remembered he'd lost Dave. Mr Catalogue volunteered her hooves.

'They're pretty sharp, you know!'

Mr Catalogue worked fast and soon they were climbing up their potato ladder and out of the pit. They'd escaped, but they were still far from home.

'If only we had Clunkalot,' said Louis, 'we could've been back in just a day or two. Poor Clunkie.' He missed his faithful

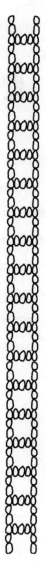

189

horse. He was really upset that he'd been turned into evil Stompalot. Louis vowed to get him back and make him good again.

'I suppose what we need are some normal, non-robot horses,' said Louis.

Mr Catalogue was worried. 'We'll need a few pennies for that. They bain't cheap!'

'I don't have a penny left,' said Louis. 'We can't walk home. It'll take weeks . . . months . . . and by then who knows what'll have happened at Castle Sideways! Maybe we can earn some money somehow?'

They jogged around the town of Chewing Grunderpips looking for anyone advertising for work. As they ran, they

passed a horse merchant. 'Oh no! Even with a steady job, it'll take weeks to raise that money!' said Louis, shaking his head in dismay. Then Mr

Catalogue pointed to a sign in a shop window nearby. It looked rather old and read, 'Barista wanted'.

'What's a bar-is-sta?' said Mr Catalogue. 'Some flavour of lawyer?'

'No, that's a barrister,' said Louis, who sometimes liked to read the dictionary before bedtime. 'A *barista* makes coffee!'

'That's all right then,' said Mr Catalogue, who quickly pulled on the time shoes and walked back a step. She disappeared.

Louis gasped, 'Oh no! Now where's she gone?'

'I'm here!' said a voice, and he turned to see someone that looked a lot like Mr Catalogue, except trimmer and fitter. She was standing in the doorway of the coffee shop.

'What happened?' said Louis. 'Where on earth did you go?'

'Didn't go nowheres!' said Mr Catalogue proudly. 'I went back in times, but stayed right

here. I walked back way too fars to begin with. Ended up surrounded by dinosaurs and volcano-no-noes. So I walks forward again and ends up here but six months ago. That's when they was first needing a barista! I was planning on trundling back to tell you what I was doing, but I tripped. Them time hoofies fell off and disappeared who-knows-when. So anyways, I volunteers for the job and they says, "yes please!" And I works for them every day and puts my pennies aside. Eventually, them all add up to some lovely gold coins for horseys.'

'Amazing!' said Louis. 'You look like a different boar!'

Mr Catalogue smiled and nodded, 'Well, I soon figures that six months grinding and squirting coffee ain't going to make me any fitter for a fight at Castle Sideways. So I is running to work, then running on the spot while I'm working, then running home afters. I'm fit as fifteen fiddlesticks now.'

Knight Sir Louis gave Mr Catalogue a big hug and they laughed for two minutes five and a half seconds. Then they walked down the road to the horse merchant.

They bought his two fastest stallions. They got a very good price because the horse merchant was a regular customer at the coffee shop.

CHAPTER 40

Knight Sir Louis and Mr Catalogue rode home as fast as they could. They only stopped for quick meals and brief sleeps. When their stallions grew tired, they traded them for fresh horses and rode on. When those horses grew tired they traded them for cows and rode them instead. When the cows grew tired they traded them for kangaroos and bounced for two days in their pouches. When the kangaroos grew tired they traded them for a tandem bicycle. When the bicycle grew tired they traded it for a hundred weasels that pulled them

along in a chariot. When the weasels grew tired they traded them for two stallions again. At last, they arrived in the kingdom of Squirrel Helm. This was a big relief for Knight Sir Louis. He didn't think arriving home on a chariot pulled by weasels was the right entrance for a hero.

Before heading for Castle Sideways, Louis found a messenger. He sent him off with two messages: one for his mum, Trixie, and one for Mysto.

Then the intrepid duo rode on towards Castle Sideways. Unfortunately, Bazooka Harry had arrived long before. Louis and Mr Catalogue trotted past a milestone: 'Castle. 3 Miles'. Above the milestone was a wonky poster on a pole.

OH YAY!
OH YAY!
LISTEN UP YOU LOT!
I AM BAZOOKA HARRY.
THE NEW KING OF
CASTLE SIDEWAYS.
IF YOU DON'T DO WHAT
I TELL YOU I WILL TURN
YOU INTO A GREASY PARSNIP
... AND I HATE PARSNIPS!
HERE ARE
MY RULES
YOU MUST OBEY ME AT ALL TIMES
YOU MUST CALL ME KING BAZOOKA
YOU MUST ALL BE IN BED BY 7 O' CLOCK
YOU MUST GIVE ME ALL YOUR MONEY
YOU MUST NOT GROW PARSNIPS
ALSO, POTATOES ARE ALL MINE!

Knight Sir Louis thought about his adventures so far. He had defeated a giant robotic Damsel. He had turned an evil dwarf back into a good dwarf. He had escaped from an underground prison. But something told him his greatest battle lay ahead.

'Come on!' said Louis to his friend, Mr Catalogue. 'We've got a castle to save!'

And now, with all the latest events, the Dark Ages News Team, with Lady Shufflepaper and Squire Chattymouth.

LS: Hello and welcome. The land of Squirrel Helm is in the news again this century.

SC: The monarch of Squirrel Helm was King Burt the Not Bad until earlier this week.

LS: This is his castle, Castle Sideways. And yes, it really is sideways.

SC: The new king is the evil wizard, Bazooka Harry, assisted by his faithful champion the Stripy Knight. The fate of King Burt is unknown at this time.

LS: Some reports say King Bazooka used Potato Magic to take over the kingdom.

SC: Over now to Magic Correspondent, Daniel Wigglewand. Daniel . . . is there such a thing as Potato Magic?

DW: Thank you for asking, Gerald. Surprisingly, there is. Some wizards have spent years trying to use all kinds of vegetables for magical purposes. Most are

not magical at all. Onions, leeks, parsnips,
turnips. A few have mild powers like the
beetroot, known for its magical ability
to turn your tongue purple, and sprouts,
known for making noxious whiffs. But the
potato can be very powerful in the right
hands . . . or the wrong hands, I should
say. There is no good magic in a potato.
It's all nasty magic, which is why the best
thing is to boil them and mash with plenty
of butter.

LS: And now some breaking news. We hear
that plucky young wizentor Pearlin is
reported missing from Castle Sideways.
Reports also indicate that King Bazooka is
hopping mad about it.

SC: In other wizentor news, the famous
Mysto has turned good again. Yesterday
he opened a new school called The Wizard
Inventor Technical college, or TWIT for
short.

END OF NEWS FLASH!

BING-A LING-A LING
DUM BONG DUM BONG

CHAPTER 41

Knight Sir Louis and Mr Catalogue gazed towards Castle Sideways.

'I hope King Burt the Not Bad is still alive,' said Louis.

What he really needed to find out was: WHAT happened WHEN, and to WHOM, and HOW badly! Then he could make a plan to take back the castle. He needed a witness. Someone who had been there when Bazooka took control. As he pondered this, a drove of donkeys walked towards them.

One of the donkeys came alongside Louis' stallion. Instead of braying, the donkey said, 'Oi! Psst!'

Most donkeys don't say things like this. Not unless they are particularly rude.

'Is that, like, really you, Knight Sir Louis?' asked the donkey.

'Er . . . yes,' said Louis, wondering if he'd lost his marbles. 'Since when do donkeys speak?' he asked.

'It's Pearlin, right!' said the donkey, as a flap flipped up on its back. It wasn't a real donkey, but a kind of clockwork, mechanical pantomime donkey with a girl inside it. It was Louis' good friend, Pearlin the wizentor.

CHAPTER 42

A short while later Louis, Mr Catalogue and Pearlin sat together in a cave. The other donkeys (real ones) and the two horses grazed at the mouth of the cave.

'He's got spies all over the place,' explained Pearlin.

'But who would want to spy for a  meanie like Bazooka Harry?' asked Louis.

'Taters,' said Pearlin.

'Taters? What's that?' asked Mr Catalogue.

'A tater is a potato,' explained Louis. 'It's just how they pronounce it in Larrrrrndun where Pearlin's from.'

'Right . . .' continued Pearlin. 'He's stuck magic taters all over. And everyone knows taters have got lots of little eyes,' she said.

This is true. Sort of. Look it up.

Pearlin continued, 'What them taters see, so can Bazooka, do you know what I mean? That's why I'm in disguise, yeah? Also, I'm using these real donkeys to, like, munch up his taters when we find 'em. Recycling them, if you know what I mean.'

Pearlin laughed. Then she offered Louis and

Mr Catalogue a special pair of spectacles each.

'Try these,' she said. 'My new invention. You can watch my memories like they was your own. I call them Memspex! Sweet name, yeah?'

Louis and Mr Catalogue popped them on.

WHOOMP!

FLASHBACK

Louis looked around. He felt just like he was standing in the castle at night. Wow! These Memspex were amazing!

He heard a strange whinnying noise and looked up. Bazooka Harry and his Stripy Knight flew down on Stompalot. Louis watched as the castle guards ran out and the huge Stripy Knight clonked each one on the head. Louis was a little embarrassed to see that the Stripy Knight was using Dave to knock them all out.

Somehow, I must get Dave back, thought Louis.

The Stripy Knight led the way up to King Burt's chamber. Bazooka followed, firing off his magical bazooka here and there. Louis watched helplessly. It was very frustrating. He wanted to stop it all happening, but of course it was just a memory, so he couldn't do a thing! AAGH!

Bazooka Harry burst into King Burt's bedroom.

'I say! Do you mind?!' said the outraged King Burt.

'No, I don't!' barked Bazooka before firing off a bolt of magic. It hit King Burt full in the

chest and a second later he sprouted green leaves from his head. Within moments poor King Burt had fully transformed into a giant parsnip. His crown was pushed off and clattered to the stone

flagstones. Bazooka picked it up and, very slowly, very importantly, put it on his own head. Louis had seen enough. He took off the Memspex.

'I saw it all,' said Pearlin. 'I wanted to stop 'em but it was, like, a total surprise. After, Bazooka comes out and tells us all he's the new king 'cause he walloped the old king.'

'He's right, too,' said Louis. 'The old laws do say that . . . but then they *were* written by King Nigel the Lunatic.'

YE OLDE LAWS OF SQUIRREL HELM Scroll 54

RULE 236: Every Thursday in a leap year will be called a Thoooosday.

RULE 237: Anyone found whistling in the castle will have their lips painted blue for a year.

RULE 238: Prisoners who can juggle five firesticks are to be pardoned (and sent to the Royal Circus).

RULE 239: If you wallop the old king until he is a goner, then you shall become the new king. Congratulations, Your Majesty.

'Them are some pretty weird rules,' agreed Mr Catalogue.

'I've really let people down,' said Louis.

'Don't go blaming yourself,' said Pearlin. 'You're

alive and that's the main thing, right? Everyone thought you was a goner. Without you, nobody wanted to fight back! But I knew you'd turn up.'

Pearlin smiled and jabbed Louis in his side with her fake donkey leg. Louis smiled. Pearlin's faith in him meant a lot.

'Well, I'm not surprised you got away either,' said Louis with a grin, then asked, 'but what about King Burt?'

'Well I smuggled him out of the castle on some donkeys, right?'

Pearlin rapped her knuckles on the rock they were sitting on. Louis and Mr Catalogue looked down and realized it wasn't a rock at all, but a very large and long parsnip. They were sitting on the king.

Knight Sir Louis stood up immediately and bowed low.

'Sorry, Your Majesty!'

'It's no use talking to it,' said Pearlin. 'He's a parsnip, yeah? I've been working on an undoing spell. But it's a bad curse, Louis. Never seen nothing like it!'

Louis slammed his fist into his palm. It was time to end this nonsense. Time to fight back. Time to defeat the Stripy Knight, King Bazooka and anyone else that wanted to cause trouble. Time to reclaim his faithful horse, Clunkalot. Time to take back his sword. Time to put King Burt back on the throne. Only one thing remained to be done before he launched his assault.

What exciting thing was this?

Well, he was going to . . .

GOING TO . . .

Er . . .

. . . go to sleep.

CHAPTER 43

Knight Sir Louis hadn't slept properly for days. (It's hard to sleep while riding a kangaroo, you know!) If he was going to take on King Bazooka he needed to be completely rested.

He had a few strange dreams. In the first he was chasing his lost sword, Dave, but never quite caught up. Then there was a dream with a huge tube of treacle. In the third there was a walrus baking a potato. In the fourth dream, or nightmare I should say, there was a wasp. That one woke Louis up. But afterwards he settled down and had a long dreamless sleep. Phew!

CHAPTER 44

Louis woke just before nightfall, feeling very refreshed.

'Here's the plan,' he said to his friends.

Pearlin and Mr Catalogue listened patiently. The plan sounded risky. But they both believed in Knight Sir Louis. They also chipped in with their own ideas, and soon they had the best plan for taking back a castle ever invented! (Well, the best one invented by a knight, a wizentor and a talking boar anyway!)

This is what happened . . .

CHAPTER 45

The sun dipped below the horizon. The donkeys wandered back towards the hill where Castle Sideways stood (or stood sideways anyway).

The evil potato spies of King Bazooka watched the donkeys closely. A number of potato spies had failed to return once again. The spies had a nasty suspicion the donkeys were responsible somehow. They noticed that one of the donkeys was unusually small.

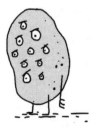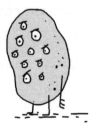

MUST BE
A FOAL.

THEY'RE ALL
FOOLS.

NO, NOT FOOL! FOAL!
AS IN BABY DONKEY.

OH, RIGHT, YEAH. I KNEW THAT.
I'M CLEVER ME. I'M NO FOAL.

218

The evil potato spies lost interest and didn't notice the little donkey walking into a cave at the foot of the hill.

But it wasn't a foal. Or a fool. It was a boar. It was Mr Catalogue wearing some donkey ears. She was looking for the secret way into the castle.

Once safely inside the cave, Mr Catalogue removed her fake ears. She was whispering to herself in the gloom.

'Made it! Phew! Now, find the steps, go up, through the ice store, into the kitchen . . . then find pots and fire and water and make steam. Steam. Steam. Steam. Gotta make steam.'

Stage One of the plan seemed to be going really well. The hardest bit – avoiding the potato spies – had gone smoothly. Mr Catalogue tiptoed towards the stone stairs.

Unfortunately, one evil potato spy, who was particularly small, knobbly and disliked by the other spies, had been sulking in the cave when Mr Catalogue wandered in.

Mr Catalogue didn't notice it in the dark, but it certainly noticed her. It smirked a horrible, potatoey smirk, showing rows of yellow-white potatoey teeth. It couldn't wait to get one over on the other potatoes. Mr Catalogue started the long climb up the stone steps. The lone potato rolled after her and kept to the shadows.

CHAPTER 46

As the moon rose, it lit the winding path to the castle. A herd of donkeys were grazing along the path. One of them had two voices. It didn't look quite right. It was a bit shonky.

'Budge up a bit!'

'I can't, can I? This thing's only supposed to fit one person.'

It was Pearlin's pretend donkey and both she and Knight Sir Louis were squeezed inside. They wandered up the path towards the royal stables by the castle walls.

In the first stall was a chestnut mare. In the next was a grey stallion. Next was an enormous bright yellow squirrel. Interesting. But nothing to do with this story.

In the last stall was another horse: broad, silver and steely. Stompalot. His eyes glowed red and steam billowed from his nose. He looked very frightening. Unfortunately, some steam also

billowed from his bottom which ruined the effect a bit. He looked with suspicion at the shonky donkey.

Stompalot thought, *I might have to trample this donkey, or boil it with nose steam. Yeah!*

But before Stompalot could decide what to do, the donkey opened its mouth.

Inside the pretend donkey, Pearlin was furiously plugging in cables here, there and everywhere. She turned dials, pressed buttons and cranked levers.

'OK, Stage Two,' whispered Knight Sir Louis.

'Microphone and speaker ready,' whispered Pearlin, and flicked a switch.

Stompalot looked into the donkey's open mouth. Instead of a tongue, there was a little, round speaker.

'If we can't bypass Stompalot's evil brain,' said Pearlin, 'we'll be donkey toast!'

Stompalot drew closer, his hot steamy breath pumping into the cramped interior of the fake donkey. Pearlin handed Louis a card.

'Here goes!' Louis said. He began reading aloud, 'Hee-haw! Haw-hee-haw! Hee-hee-hee-hee-haw!'

OH NO! LOUIS' LOST IT! HE'S GONE BONKERS AND STARTED TALKING LIKE A DONKEY.

HANG ON! MAYBE IT'S SOME KIND OF CUNNING PLAN.

OH, YES.

MAYBE STOMPALOT UNDERSTANDS DONKEY LANGUAGE.

YES! OF COURSE! I WONDER WHAT HE'S SAYING?

LET'S GET BETTY THE TRANSLATOR. SHE SPEAKS ELEVENTY LANGUAGES.

OH, YES, QUITE SIMPLE REALLY. THE TRANSLATION IS... HEY, STOMPALOT, TIME TO REBOOT YOUR LAMPSHADE!

← BETTY

EH? THAT DOESN'T MAKE ANY SENSE.

UH-OH! SOUNDS LIKE LOUIS' SAID THE WRONG THING. HE'S IN TROUBLE NOW!

225

Pearlin and Louis coughed as Stompalot snorted a huge burst of steam inside their donkey disguise.

'We're goners!' said Pearlin. 'He didn't reboot!'

Stompalot reared up and kicked with his front hooves. He burst out of his stable in a salvo of splintered wood and iron nails. He pounded a sparking hoof on the cobbles and let out a great whinny that sounded like a hundred wild and angry beasts all screaming together.

'He's going to make mincemeat of us!' shrieked Pearlin in a panic.

But Louis kept calm. He checked the words on the card again.

'Whoops!' he said. 'I used a hee-hee instead of a hee-haw.'

Stompalot reared up again and prepared to box the fake donkey to the ground with his mighty, metal hooves.

'HEE-HAW! HAW-HEE-HAW! HEE-HEE-HAW! HEE-HAW!' shouted Louis.

AH. THAT MAKES MUCH MORE SENSE.
THE NEW TRANSLATION IS...
HEY, STOMPALOT, TIME TO
REBOOT YOUR COMPUTER!

Stompalot paused in the exact second before crushing the donkey. He lowered his front legs to the ground. The glow in his eyes faded. His head dropped.

'Did it work?' asked Knight Sir Louis.

Suddenly, Stompalot's head flicked back up and he opened his mouth wide. He coughed and spat out the evil magic potato that Bazooka had put inside his brain box. It landed on the cobbles with a fat splat. Immediately the horse's eyes started to glow again, but this time they were a calm green.

'SUCCESS!' shouted Pearlin.

'That's my Clunkalot!' shouted Knight Sir Louis, overjoyed.

Louis leapt out of the pretend donkey, rushed to the restored Clunkalot and threw his arms around his metal neck. Clunkie nudged his friend with his long, metal nose. He was so glad to be free of the horrible controller that had turned him into Bazooka's slave. He composed a poem especially for the moment:

When you're not yourself
ask friends to find a new path
back to who you are.

Bit of a soppy one, but Clunkie was feeling quite emotional, and anyway, it's good to express your feelings. This isn't the Dark Ages you know!

CHAPTER 47

Stage Two wasn't easy. But it made Stage Three look like a walk in the meadow. Stage Three was 'find and defeat the Stripy Knight'.

Knight Sir Louis climbed inside Clunkalot. Pearlin climbed back into the shonky donkey. Together they clip-clopped their way through the castle gates. Just a horse and a donkey. Nothing

unusual. Some evil potato spies noticed them. They were suspicious but couldn't put their fingers on why (this isn't surprising as potatoes do have eyes but don't have fingers).

The horse and donkey clip-clopped over the drawbridge. The courtyard was quiet. The merchants and their customers were gone, scared off by the new king. But it wasn't entirely empty. There was a tall guard box and inside, standing very still, was the Stripy Knight. Hanging from his belt was the sword, Dave.

Now, let's go inside the mind of the Stripy Knight. You may be wondering what a person made of potatoes thinks about. Well, here's what the Stripy Knight was thinking right then:

I like soil, soil, soil. Hey! Isn't that Stompalot out of his stable? . . . I like soil.

Then the Stripy Knight saw the donkey and thought:

I hate worms, worms, worms. Hey! What's a donkey doing here? Don't they eat potatoes? GRRR! . . . I hate worms . . . and donkeys!

Pearlin's shonky donkey came close to the Stripy Knight, pretending to sniff for snacks on the ground. Then she turned as if to walk away. The Stripy Knight considered giving the donkey a kick in the behind. But the donkey beat him to it. Pearlin kicked out a back leg and hit the Stripy Knight in the chest, then ran off.

Enraged, the Stripy Knight unsheathed his sword and started to chase the donkey. Louis followed in Clunkalot. They ran around the courtyard twice, then ran straight into the castle kitchens.

And this had been Louis' plan all along! By now Mr Catalogue would have filled the kitchens with steam. Louis guessed that since the Stripy Knight was made of potato he would be cooked into mash by all the steam. HA!

But as they raced into the kitchen, Louis saw something was wrong. There was no steam. Not one single pot on the boil. What had happened to Mr Catalogue?

CHAPTER 48

WHAT HAPPENED TO MR CATALOGUE

As you may remember, Mr Catalogue had slipped into the castle through a secret path. And she wasn't alone as an evil potato spy had followed  her. What happened next was reported later on an Accident Form prepared by Castle Sideways' chief nurse, Matron O'Goole. Matron likes to read gothic novels, as you will see:

YE ACCIDENT FORM

'Twas a dark and moonless night when the talking boar came unto the cave. Lo, she found the black and glistening staircase foretold by the mysterious knight. The boar wondered if she was truly alone. Was that a sound behind her? Each time she did look, there was nothing to see but darkness.

Ooool

The steps beneath her trotters were wet with moisture dripping from the stalactites above. She saw them hanging like weird teeth and she did quiver.

Ohhh!

Little did she know a malevolent creature WAS with her. 'Twas . . . a nasty potato. And it did bounce ahead of the boar and put itself under her trotter.

Oh! Oh! Oh!

Down the poor boar did fall, bumping her head against the hard, cruel floor of the cave. She was knocked out all of a sudden (and suffered a minor cut which I later cleaned and stitched).

Fie! Fie!

Meanwhile, it is to be imagined, the evil potato did snigger and tell itself it was a terrible genius. Surely it must have wished to tell its devilish comrades what it had done and earn their admiration. But alas and alack and alas once more. For the vibrations of the boar's fall did cause a thin, sharp stalactite to break from the cave roof. Down it came like the curse of a mighty spirit and, by total coincidence, it did spear the evil potato right through its middle. (There was nothing I could do to save it. I'm a nurse not a gardener.)

REPORT ENDS.

235

Anyway, when Mr Catalogue awoke, she wasn't sure where she was. She felt the bump on her head.

Ow! Then remembered why she was there!

'Oh, noses!' she said to herself. 'How long have I been all knocked out and lying around?'

She raced up the steps as fast as she could. At the top she found an oval wooden door with a latch. Very carefully she opened it and stepped through. She found herself amongst a pile of massive ice cubes. She had broken into the ice room!

She shivered and thought to herself, *I better not hangs about or I'll be a pig popsicle.*

She slid and slipped across the blocks of ice to the other side where she opened a second door into the wide kitchen. Finally things were going to plan! Except they weren't, because she could hear Clunkalot, the donkey and the Stripy Knight clattering down the corridor towards her. They would be there at any moment and she hadn't time to make any steam!

She raced around looking for pots. But then she opened a kitchen cupboard and found something else.

'Oo!' said Mr Catalogue.

Maybe she wouldn't need steam after all!

Now, you're wondering what this 'thing' was, right? Well, here's the advert for it seen in popular magazine 'Castle Cookery for Castle Cooks'.

CHAPTER 49

The donkey (containing Pearlin), Clunkalot (containing Louis) and the Stripy Knight (containing a string of enchanted potatoes) raced into the kitchen.

The Stripy Knight leapt and swung from an iron chandelier. He swept down and landed a kick on the donkey. With a swift slice of his sword he cut off the donkey's head! Pearlin was lucky her head wasn't chopped off with it. She pressed the emergency exit button and was ejected

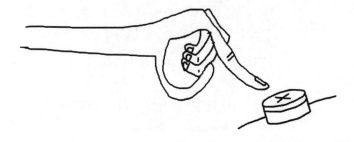

from a flap in the donkey's bum.

Meanwhile, Knight Sir Louis had a new plan. Stage Three, Version Two went into effect immediately.

The Stripy Knight heard a strange whirring noise. It came from Clunkalot's tail. It was spinning around like a giant fan and very soon created a gale force wind.

Meanwhile, the Stripy Knight was thinking, *I like damp, dark soil. But I'm going off Stompalot. Maybe he's a potato muncher?*

The Stripy Knight was struggling to stay still as the force of Clunkie's gale grew stronger. The Stripy Knight wasn't going to stand for this. He took out the sword Dave and managed to lift it unsteadily.

Pearlin looked up from where she'd landed. She shook her head in dismay. 'Run, Louis! The sword!'

But this was precisely what Knight Sir Louis had hoped for. As soon as the Stripy Knight lifted Dave into the rushing wind, his blade started to vibrate, and then hum, and then SING! And we all know what happens when Dave starts singing . . .

The sound was so awful, so phenomenally ear-dribblingly bad, that the Stripy Knight forgot

what he was doing. He didn't even notice a whole
herd of walruses come flopping into the kitchen.

'What splendid music,' said one walrus to
another in walrus language.

'Such an exquisite tone,' replied the other.

In no time they had surrounded the Stripy
Knight and Clunkie and were happily honking
and burping along with the horrible music,
making the sound even more unpleasant (if that
was possible).

The Stripy Knight couldn't stand it any more.
He let go of Dave and the sword flew away in the

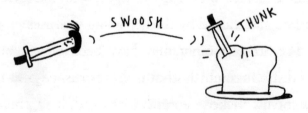

SWOOSH

THUNK

gale. It landed, shuddering, in a thick loaf of bread. The sword's song stopped. This really annoyed the walruses who thought the concert had come to an end far too early. They barked and moaned and starting poking the Stripy Knight with their long tusks.

This gave Louis the chance he'd hoped for. He jumped out of Clunkalot, ran and took back his sword. HOORAY! He drew Dave from the loaf of bread, rather like when King Arthur took his sword from a stone (except this was a lot easier). Then he turned to face the Stripy Knight who was being pushed and shoved by the departing walruses.

The Stripy Knight may have been bigger, but he wasn't as nimble as Louis. Louis rushed over to his enemy, flicked out with his sword, here, there, under there, round here, up there, back and forth and then stood back.

CLANG!
BONG!
TING!

The Stripy Knight's armour fell off in chunks exposing the string of potatoes inside. But even then the Stripy Knight wasn't about to give up the fight. He still wore one of his big gauntlets. He

grabbed Knight Sir Louis, squeezing him so hard
he had to drop Dave.

CLATTER!

Then the Stripy Knight threw Louis hard across
the room.

WHOOSH

He landed against a cupboard.

The Stripy Knight ran over for another go. The cupboard door beside Louis popped open to reveal Mr Catalogue. She handed over the huge grater she'd found.

'Hey-ho! Better late than never, eh? Anyways, I found this thingy in here. Want it?'

'Oo! Yes please!' said Louis.

The Stripy Knight hurled himself up onto the chandelier again. He swung and dropped. He was going to come down full force on Louis. But then Louis lifted up the giant cheese grater. There was nothing the potatoey Stripy Knight could do. He hit it and went straight through . . . sliced into very neat French fries.

And that was the end of the Stripy Knight.

Pearlin rushed over to give Louis and Mr Catalogue a high five each.

'Oo! Ouch!' said Pearlin, remembering too late that Knight Sir Louis wore metal gauntlets and Mr Catalogue had sharp hooves.

'Stage Three complete!' said Louis happily.

Before Stage Four they decided to eat something to keep their strength up. They had French fries.

CHAPTER 50

Stage Four of the plan was on. Mr Catalogue, Clunkalot, Louis and Pearlin hid behind some stone columns in the Great Hall.

They spied on the entrance to a wide spiral stairwell. It led up the tower to the king's chambers. Getting up there wasn't going to be easy. Every stair was lined with evil potato spies. And at the

bottom of the stairs they crowded together in a great semi-circle, like a barricade of balls.

'We're going to have to mash our way through those potatoes first,' said Louis.

Mr Catalogue rubbed the bump on her head. 'It's not going to be easy peasies,' she said.

'We need to lure them out,' said Louis, 'trap them somehow.'

Pearlin smiled. 'Whoa! I've got an idea. Get them to my lab and it'll be like splat city.'

'Nice!' said Louis.

Pearlin sneaked off.

'But how is we going to get the potatoes out?' asked Mr Catalogue.

'My plan is . . . we really annoy them,' said Louis.

'Oo! I volunteers for that,' said Mr Catalogue. 'You stay heres and hide. I'll get them down to Pearlin's place.'

Louis gave Mr Catalogue some quick directions to the lab, then he and Clunkie watched as Mr Catalogue put on her fake donkey ears and

trotted over to the horde of evil potatoes. They turned towards her and squinted with deep suspicion.

'Hey yous!' she shouted at them. 'You potato chumps! Want to know who I am? I'm the tiny donkey queen, yeah. That's right. I'm the one who's been telling donkeys to munch up any potatoes they see. Ha ha! You lumps of . . . erm . . . starch!'

Knight Sir Louis tried not to laugh. He watched as the evil potato spies started bouncing up and down with rage.

'Anytime we see a potato,' said Mr Catalogue, 'we get the munchies. What do you think about that?'

The potatoes pushed each other out of the way to get closer to Mr Catalogue.

'We can't get enough,' she said. 'Munch crunch. Lovely lunch. Oo, we've had mash, chips, fries, crisps, roasties, boiled, baked, sauté, rösti, dauphinoise, Lyonnaise, hash browns, au gratin, skins, croquettes . . .'

The potatoes were furious. They flipped and leapt like popping corn. They tumbled themselves in a vegetable avalanche towards Mr Catalogue.

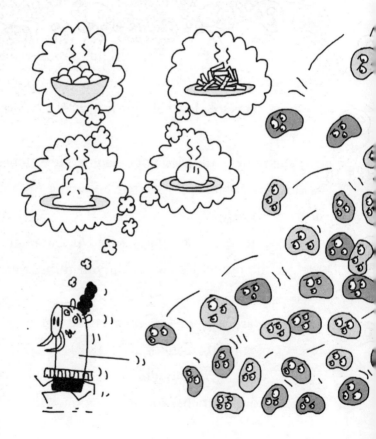

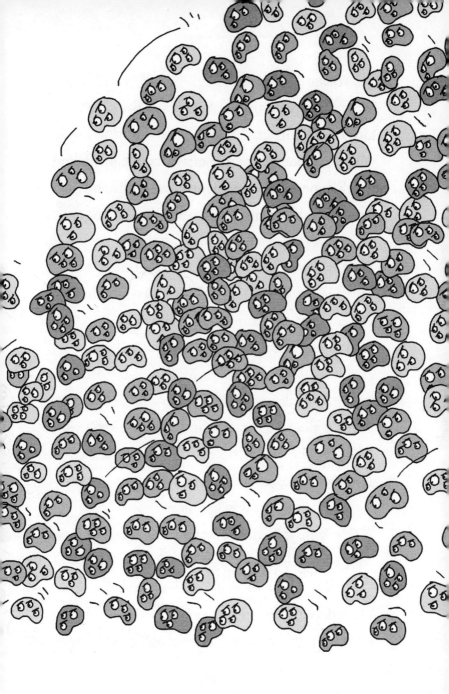

'Uh-oh!' she said.

She turned and ran for it. They followed, determined to exact revenge on the tiny donkey queen. Louis thought she was going to make it. But Clunkalot was watching too and doing some quick calculations. He worked out there was a 90% probability that Mr Catalogue would be caught by the potatoes. Mr Catalogue hadn't done any calculations, but looking over her shoulder, she came to the same conclusion.

'Uh oh! Clunkie! Over 'ere,' she called out.

Clunkalot leapt out, barrelled Mr Catalogue onto his back and rode off towards Pearlin's lab. Mr Catalogue gave a thumbs (or trotters) up to Louis as she was whisked away. The huge pile of potatoes followed as she rode Clunkie out of the Great Hall. Louis was left alone.

He scurried up the stairs and, at last, found himself outside the king's chambers.

The moment of truth had arrived. Louis was excited but also a little worried. Bazooka Harry wasn't your everyday, bog-standard villain. He was cunning and ruthless. He had already tricked Louis once. Louis looked at himself in the long hall mirror and wondered how he could be sure he wasn't walking straight into another trap.

CHAPTER 51.

You may be wondering what King Bazooka had been doing all this time . . .

NOT REALLY.   I WAS.   WAS HE AT THE HAIRDRESSERS?

King Bazooka was not at the hairdressers. He was having a bath (still wearing his crown, of course). He'd heard rumours and whisperings. His subjects had taken to calling him King Stink and King Whiff and, worst of all, King Pong. He'd overheard one of the guards saying that the new king smelt of hot mud and cow dung. That was shortly before the guard had been magically bazookered and turned into a pile of roast parsnips.

King Bazooka was cleaning his fingernails with a wire brush and some lavender soap when he heard something . . . a clatter and a bang outside his chambers. He sloshed out of his bath, dressed in a towelling robe and stepped into his soft

slippers. Last, but not least, he strapped the magical bazooka onto his back. He crept to the main door to his chambers. He peered through the peephole to see if anyone was waiting in the hall.

And there he was!

Knight Sir Louis!

Somehow Louis had escaped his prison and made it here. King Bazooka was almost pleased about it. He would now have the pleasure of defeating this pesky knight a second time. King Bazooka got ready. Three, two, one. He flung open the door, aimed the crosshairs of the magical bazooka at Louis' helmet. And fired.

The smoke cleared. Where Knight Sir Louis had been there was now just a crumpled bent heap of metal, cinders and yes, parsnips. Knight Sir Louis was a goner.

King Bazooka stepped up to the pile of ashes and vegetables that used to be Knight Sir Louis. He laughed with his horrible hissy laugh, 'HSSSSSSS—' Well, you know how it goes.

It was the best moment ever in King Bazooka's whole life!

Then, mid-hiss, he stopped. In amongst the vegetables and ashes was something else. Something shiny. And it wasn't pieces of armour . . . it was shards of a mirror! He suddenly had the feeling that someone was standing right behind him.

He was right. Someone was . . .

A-HA! IT WAS A TRICK WITH A MIRROR RIGHT?

THAT'S WHAT BAZOOKA HARRY BLASTED. LOUIS WASN'T STANDING THERE AT ALL.

CLEVER.

Knight Sir Louis!

Louis felt really good! He had played Bazooka at his own game. He'd laid a trap and King Bazooka had walked right into it. King Bazooka fell back and lifted his bazooka once more, but Louis was ready. He slashed up with Dave and cut the magical bazooka in two. But the bazooka was full of stored magic and now it needed somewhere to go. It backfired into Bazooka Harry himself.

KABOOM!

Louis watched, amazed and disgusted, as King Bazooka's body bubbled and wobbled and grew.

'WHAT HAVE YOU DONE TO ME?' shouted King Bazooka, as he transformed into a

very knobbly man-sized potato. His body swelled while his arms and legs became even more spindly than before. Yes, a man-sized potato is a strange thing to behold. Even more strange is a man-sized potato wearing a bathrobe and slippers.

King Bazooka reached out to grab his enemy but Louis ducked just in time. King Bazooka hit the door instead and it turned into a weird potatoey sludge. Raw potato magic was flowing out of King Bazooka now.

King Bazooka tried to strike again. Louis

ducked a second time. King Bazooka hit the walls of the tower instead. The stones turned into potato gloop and dribbled away. This left a big hole in the wall. And as King Bazooka lurched at Louis a third time, they both slipped on the gloop. King Bazooka and Louis fell through the hole. Louis reached out and grabbed an edge and clung on for dear life. King Bazooka wasn't as lucky. He tried to hold on, but his huge potato body weighed him down. His fingers slipped and he fell down, down,

down into the mud below. SPLAT!

This was just about the same time that the potato spies chasing Mr Catalogue and Clunkalot arrived in Pearlin's lab. Pearlin was waiting for them. She opened the big delivery hatch in the wall of her lab. The potato spies tumbled out, thudding onto the ground far below.

Mr Catalogue, Pearlin and Clunkalot sighed with relief. Phew! But Clunkie wasn't about to rest up. He'd been worrying about Louis. He launched himself out of the hatch and spread his mechanical wings. He flew up to the top end of the castle and caught sight of Louis hanging on for dear life.

'Am I glad to see you!' said Louis as Clunkalot hovered beneath him. Louis let go and landed on Clunkie's back.

'Yes! Now let's find Bazooka,' said Louis. 'I want to make sure we've won.'

They flew low. All seemed quiet.

For a moment.

But then they saw him. The weird potato man that was King Bazooka stood up, covered in mud, and ran towards the pile of potato spies. He dived inside the pile.

What's he doing? wondered Louis.

A moment later they knew. The pile of potatoes glowed and reshaped and reformed into one giant blob.

More nasty magic, thought Louis.

And then it solidified into an enormous potato waffle with arms and legs. Bazooka's evil eyes gazed out from the top of the waffle. It stood up and roared.

'Not something you see every day,' gulped Mr Catalogue who was watching the action unfold from Pearlin's lab.

Louis gasped. Things were going from bad to worse. He tried to come up with another plan. But he hadn't thought anything this bonkers would happen. He'd come home to Castle Sideways hoping to save the day, to be the great hero! But now it looked like he might have made things a hundred times worse. He wasn't going to give up. The only thing left to do was a direct attack on the Giant Waffle. It seemed hopeless, but he'd run out of options.

Louis raised his sword and called out, 'Hear me, great foe! I am Knight Sir Louis, defender and champion of the people! Prepare to fight! YAH!'

Louis and Clunkalot soared through the air, diving heroically towards the Giant Waffle. It roared and prepared to swat Louis and Clunkalot into oblivion. Then Louis heard another deep booming noise. He turned his head and saw . . . oh no!

The Damsel of Distresse was back.

Louis was stuck between two terrible foes. He watched in horror as the Damsel opened her mouth and shouted.

'Hello, Poppet!'

This was not what Louis had expected. But you see, in a way, Louis had already made a plan.

I BET THIS IS SOMETHING TO DO WITH THOSE MESSAGES HE SENT TO HIS MUM AND MYSTO EARLIER.

OH YEAH!

There was only one person that called him poppet and that was his mother.

'Mum?'

'That's right,' said Trixie. 'Mysto and I got your messages. He repaired this old Damsel thing and now I'm in control. It really is a lot of fun!'

And with that, the Damsel ran towards the Giant Waffle.

This was the first (and last) time in history that a Giant Waffle fought a Giant Damsel. It did not disappoint.

269

The Giant Waffle managed to pull off one of the Damsel's arms.

But . . . the Damsel used her fireball breath to roast the middle of the waffle.

The Giant Waffle managed to twist the Damsel's head back to front.

But . . . the Damsel managed to split the Giant Waffle's top half in two with a (one-armed) karate chop.

The Giant Waffle went for a knockout blow. It prepared to ram the Damsel and knock her down. But Louis saw a chance for victory.

He and Clunkie flew in front of the Giant Waffle, distracting it for a moment. It was all Louis' mum needed. She sidestepped and stuck out a Damsel boot. The Giant Waffle tripped and fell

flat, smashing into a giant potatoey slush. The potato magic seeped away into the ground. The nasty magic was gone at last. Lying, very wet and fed up, in the middle of it all was King Bazooka, back to his human self again. Just in time too, as the Damsel's battle damage forced Trixie to shut it down.

Clunkie landed and Knight Sir Louis dismounted. He walked over to Bazooka and said, 'It's over! You're beaten!'

Bazooka was breathless and weak.

'I'm taking you to the dungeons,' said Louis.

Bazooka started to laugh.

'What's so funny?'

'We have one thing in common, you and me,' said Bazooka.

'Don't start telling me we're the same,' said Louis, who knew that all baddies liked to say this sort of thing at the end.

'But we are the same!' said Bazooka. 'Neither of us ever gives up.'

Bazooka smiled a very sinister grin and said, 'One of the best things about being King of Castle Sideways was I got to read all the Secret Service files. And I found one all about you. That's how I know your greatest fear. Ha!'

Bazooka reached up to his crown and pressed a jewel on it like it was a button!

'What have you done now?' asked Louis.

'You'll find out very soon!'

Louis heard a faint sound. A sort of fizzing. It grew louder and louder. It filled Louis with liquid dread from the tips of his toenails to the ends of his ears. The sound went like this . . .

bbbbᴠᴠᴠᴠᴜᴜᴜᴜUUUUZZZZ
ZZZZZZ!

It was a wasp.

And it was coming for Louis.

CHAPTER 52

The wasp was a normal wasp. But that's not how it seemed to Louis in his terror. He imagined the

wasp's horrid compound eyes like a honeycomb of dark menace. He thought of its vile, venous wings flapping a thousand times a second, creating the disgusting buzz that battered at Louis' eardrums. He shivered to think of its antennae groping the air, testing and tasting for prey. Worst of all, he imagined the sting, wicked and poisonous, with a sparkling needle point. AAGH!

Louis couldn't move. The wasp buzzed nearer and nearer. He couldn't even hold onto his sword. Dave slipped from his fingers and thudded into the earth.

Bazooka laughed his hissing laugh and said, 'It's true! It's true! You ARE afraid of wasps!'

Clunkalot was desperate to help, but he'd landed in the potatoey gloop and it had temporarily stuck his hooves to the ground.

Bazooka grinned a horrible, wide smirk and shook his head at Louis. 'It's no good! This is the end for you, Louis. I have cursed this tiny insect with a very special spell. Whoever it stings will be transported far, far away. It will take you to its papery nest deep in the darkest mountain. It will keep you glued up there forever with a thousand of its friends. You'll never escape from its nasty, waspy, treacle-y trap!'

The wasp was flying just in front of Louis' face now. It curled its cursed sting underneath itself and reached out with its six dangling legs. But then, in the depth of his terror, one of Bazooka's words caught Louis' attention.

'TREACLE!' shouted Louis.

He remembered Mysto's gift – a squeezy tube of molasses treacle.

He felt the blood rushing into his arms and legs like hot water. He could move again!

'CLUNKIE!' he shouted to his faithful friend. 'TREACLE!'

Clunkie's mouth clanked open and the tube

of treacle fired from his mouth. Louis grabbed

it and turned to Bazooka, quick as a flash. Louis
squeezed hard on the tube and . . .

. . . the treacle squirted and landed . . .

. . . on Bazooka Harry. An instant later the
wasp, just a moment away from stinging Louis,
stopped! It seemed to be tasting the air with its

great weaving antennae. Bazooka frantically tried to wipe the treacle off his bathrobe, but instead just spread it around even more. With lightning speed the wasp caught the scent of the sugary molasses and pounced. It landed and curled its sting and . . .

'OWWWWW!'

It stung Bazooka.

'NO!' shouted Bazooka in desperation. 'YOU STUPID WASP! NOT ME!'

An instant later Bazooka Harry disappeared into thin air. The crown from his head remained and fell to the ground. It circled round and round a few times before stopping at Louis' feet.

The curse took Bazooka far away to the wasp's papery nest, deep in the darkest mountain where it lived with all its waspy friends. And do you know where this mountain was? Chapter Twenty-Eight. Go and have a look! You'll see!

CHAPTER 53

PHEW! Now that was a close thing. Bazooka was a cunning bad guy. He had a lot of tricks up his sleeve, but in the end he just wasn't smart enough for Louis. So to sum up, here's the final result:

FINAL SCORE
_____

BAZOOKA HARRY **0** **1** KNIGHT SIR LOUIS

HOORAH!

CHAPTER 54

A week later things started to return to normal. Trixie returned home the day after the battle.

'The Guild of Knights won't run itself,' she explained, giving Louis a goodbye kiss.

Word soon spread that Bazooka Harry had been defeated. The people of Squirrel Helm helped Louis, Pearlin and Mr Catalogue capture the remaining evil potato spies. And they carried the huge parsnip that used to be King Burt the Not Bad back to the castle.

Pearlin and Mysto became acquainted at last. They spent all week examining the remaining pieces of Bazooka Harry's magical bazooka. They studied it and worked out how to reverse King Burt's vegetable curse. But this raised a rather puzzling problem.

Louis had defeated King Bazooka. Therefore, according to the laws of the land, Louis was now king.

King Louis!

King Louis of Squirrel Helm.

King Louis of Castle Sideways.

Some people thought Louis should stay on as king and just forget King Burt. Being king had lots of advantages: a crown, a big comfy nine-poster bed, a bubble bath with gold flakes in it, soft llama fur pyjamas, and, of course, being able to tell everyone else what to do. He'd also found all the missing gold, silver and chocolate coins. Bazooka had brought them all back to the castle treasury when he took over as king.

But Pearlin wasn't sure Louis would like it much. She brought him a special book, given to each new king.

Louis sat and read the first few chapters. It turned out there were all kinds of downsides to

being a king. For starters, you weren't allowed to go on exciting adventures. It was important to stay indoors as much as possible. Fighting dragons was forbidden.

Adventures, being outdoors and fighting dragons were some of Louis' favourite things. Maybe being a king wasn't such a great idea?

I have to find a way of giving Burt his throne back! thought King Louis.

The only way to restore Burt was to have a fight. Burt would have to defeat King Louis (which wasn't very likely). King Louis didn't want to fight his old boss, but there didn't seem a way around it. The laws of the land were quite clear and rules were rules!

At last, Pearlin was ready to bring Burt back to life. The huge parsnip lay in the Great Hall. Pearlin aimed the magical bazooka.

'You're sure this'll work?' asked King Louis.

'About sixty two point three percent sure,' said Pearlin. 'Mysto and I hotwired the bazooka's magic capacitors to send an inverse phase loop back through the power filaments and create an antimatter flux spell which is magnified through the paranormal diodes. Simple really.'

'Mmm,' said Louis, who didn't think it sounded simple at all.

'If it don't works,' said Mr Catalogue, 'we could put old Burt in a big glass box and wait for a princess to come. Then if she falls in love with the ole parsnip she could kiss it and he'd come back to life. That's how these things work in story time.'

'Mmm,' said Louis, who didn't think it sounded like any fairy story he'd heard. The bazooka seemed to be their best chance. 'Well, do it,' said King Louis and gave the nod.

Pearlin pulled the trigger. The bazooka made a noise that started very loud and became gradually quieter and quieter.

A bolt of yellow and purple lightning flew out of the bazooka without any noise at all. It hit the parsnip. When the smoke cleared . . . Burt was back.

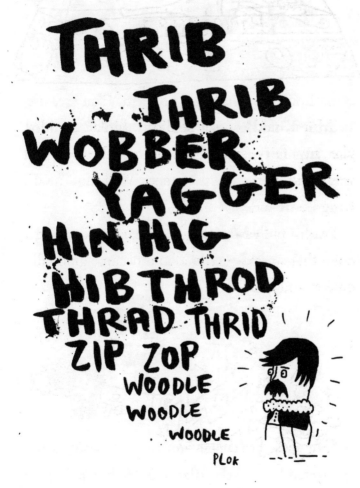

THRIB
THRIB
WOBBER
YAGGER
HIN HIG
HIB THROD
THRAD THRID
ZIP ZOP
WOODLE
WOODLE
WOODLE
PLOK

CHAPTER 55

King Louis explained the problem. 'You see, sire, because King Bazooka beat you, and I beat him, that means I'm now king. So, you have to beat me.'

'But I'm no match for your sword skills!' spluttered Burt, rather alarmed. He had just spent two weeks as a vegetable. He'd narrowly avoided being chopped up and fried. Now he was cured, but faced the possibility of being sliced up anyway!

'You could always challenge me to a different kind of competition,' hinted King Louis.

A smile spread across Burt's face. 'Oh yes!'

And so Burt challenged King Louis to a race ... on his computer. They played the racing-horse-and-cart game. King Louis played his best, but Burt beat him easily. The fact was Louis was better in real races, real battles and real death-defying situations. But Burt was better at playing and winning computer games. We all have our strengths and weaknesses.

'I'm beaten, Your Majesty,' smiled Louis, handing over the crown, 'which means you are king again!'

'And my first royal appointment,' said the new (old) King Burt, 'is to make you Deputy King. Just in case I get in trouble again.'

Clunkalot was so pleased with the way things had worked out that he wrote a new poem.

Make time for questions.
One day the answers will bloom
as happy endings.

That evening King Burt the Not Bad (officially King Burt the Not Bad the First and Second) threw a banquet. It was the finest for years and years. There was plenty of food (though it was mainly potatoes). No parsnips were cooked. In fact, from that day forward, parsnips were a protected vegetable in the land of Squirrel Helm.

King Burt gave a long speech (yawn) and presented Knight Sir Louis with a fabulous golden medal for outstanding bravery (yay!). He also gave medals to Pearlin, Clunkalot and Mr Catalogue (triple yay!).

It was a fabulous evening, but just when everyone thought the story was over, a potential sequel reared its ugly head. A messenger burst into the banqueting hall with an urgent email. King Burt read it out loud for all to hear.

King Burt! Please send help at once. A new and terrible dragon with two heads has burned the village of Little Matchstick to the ground. If it is not stopped it will eat all our animals and scorch the land!

The dragon was none other than Borax, the dragon that had eaten King Burt's brother, Prince Garibaldi! King Burt turned to his champion knight, but Knight Sir Louis was not in his seat. Neither was Mr Catalogue. They were already climbing onto trusty steed, Clunkalot.

Knight Sir Louis, Champion Knight and Deputy King of Castle Sideways of the land of Squirrel Helm raised up his mighty sword, Dave, and spoke these heroic words:

SEE YOU LATER!
SAVE ME A ROAST POTATO!

ACKNOWLEDGEMENTS

Thank you to Gaia Banks for her sage guidance and finding a home for Knight Sir Louis. Thank you to Bella Pearson for giving Clunkalot a happy stable in which to live. Thank you to Lucy Fawcett for being our ongoing champion. Thank you to Amy Dobson for being Castle Sideways' Town Crier. Thank you to Hannah Featherstone and Kathy Webb for taking turns as Squire Typo. Thanks to Colyn Allsopp for being Typeset Wizentor.

Thank you to our parents for letting us pursue artistic passions instead of making us choose a more sensible life. Thank you to Lucy and Evgenia for your constant support. Thank you to Louis for providing the original inspiration for the story and for suggesting that Bazooka Harry should (of course) have a bazooka.

Greg and Myles McLeod are known as The Brothers McLeod for two reasons. The first reason is that they have the same surname. The second reason is that they are brothers. They come up with silly stories together, then Greg draws the pictures and Myles writes the words. They have won things like a BAFTA and make cartoons for people like Disney, the Royal Shakespeare Company and the BBC.

www.bromc.uk
www.gregmcleod.uk
www.mylesmcleod.com

GUPPY
BOOKS

Guppy Books is an independent children's publisher based in Oxford in the UK, publishing exceptional fiction for children of all ages. Small and responsive, inclusive and communicative, Guppy Books was set up in 2019 and publishes only the very best authors and illustrators from around the world.

From brilliantly funny illustrated tales for five-year-olds to inspiring and thought-provoking novels for young adults, Guppy Books promises to publish something for everyone. If you'd like to know more about our authors and books, go to the Guppy Aquarium on YouTube where you'll find interviews, drawalongs and all sorts of fun.

We hope that our books bring pleasure to young people of all ages, and also to the adults sharing these books with them. Children's literature plays a part in giving both young and old the resources and reflection needed to grow up in today's ever-changing world, and we hope that you enjoy this small piece of magic!

Bella Pearson
Publisher

www.guppybooks.co.uk